A LOVER'S ORIGIN

A Ramsey Novella

A LOVER'S ORIGIN

ISBN: 9780982978122

Copyright © 2010 by AlTonya Washington

All rights reserved. No part of this book may be reproduced or transmitted in any form or by any means without written permission from the author.

This is a work of fiction. Characters, names, incidents, organizations and dialogue in this novel are either products of the author's imagination or are used fictitiously.

Printed in USA by CreateSpace

A Lover's Origin

Quaysar and Tykira

She stood there biting her thumbnail and watching him from the high arched doorway leading into the living area of the cottage. He'd acted like he'd been in another world most of the day. She figured he was finally returning to reality and asking himself what in the world he'd brought her there for.

It had been almost a week and Quay Ramsey had yet to explain why he'd taken her to his grandparent's estate on the outskirts of Savannah, Georgia. She hadn't even been aware that the place existed on the expansive

A Lover's Origin

property where Quay's uncle Houston and aunt Daphne now resided.

The trip hadn't been a waste though- not by any means. Tykira Lowery knew she'd probably be grounded for a decade when she finally got home and tried to explain to her mother where she'd been for the last three days. Whatever the outcome, she knew it'd be worth it. It'd be so worth it. She'd been in love with Quaysar Ramsey forever. Being in the same room with him was unbelievable. Being *alone* in the same room with him was heaven.

Quay stood near the stereo system shuffling through a stack of albums without really seeing the covers. He figured that he'd have at least waited until the last day; instead of the third of this grand adventure he'd planned, to start having a crisis of conscience. Long lashes settled down over the pitch darkness of his gaze as he silently cursed himself. It hadn't been necessary to go to such lengths. He didn't have to bring her there- hell, not for a damn week anyway. They'd spent the better part of their lives as friends, why the urge to change it all up now?

Because he loved her. His right dimple flashed as he grimaced over the admission. He wasn't angered by it. A guy like him had no business falling in love with a girl like Tykira Lowery. She had the body and face of a goddess and no clue how to use them to torture or tease the opposite sex. Sweetness clung to her like some sugary confection and he hadn't been immune regardless of the lies he told himself.

Now he stood there selecting music- *trying to select music* to enhance the seduction of an angel. Seduction was only part of it, of course. This seduction would be followed

A Lover's Origin

by a betrayal. A betrayal that was sure to have her hating him. Unfortunately, there was no other way. Her hating him was the only way this could work.

She cleared her throat and he smiled. All thoughts of betrayal and hatred left his mind then.

"Hey," he flashed a smile from across his shoulder as he lifted a few of the albums. "Come help me pick out some music."

Tykira smoothed a lock of hair behind her ear and joined him near the stereo. She reached for a stack of albums and giggled after she'd gone through a few.

Quay nudged her arm with his elbow. "What?"

"Just hard to believe your aunt and uncle listen to Culture Club."

"They don't." Quay laughed then too. "Lucky for us they aren't the only ones who use this place. So we've got input from folks with actual taste in music." He set Janet Jackson's *Control* album to play.

Tykira selected the Culture Club album along with two others. "So what are we doing tonight?" She asked and moved close to pat the middle of his back when he started to cough. "Are you okay?"

"Dinner." He said around another cough and nodded. "Dinner's what we're doin'. You got the taste for anything?" He'd already started for the kitchen.

"I'm not really that much of a cook Quay." She watched him open the cabinets in the small cozy kitchen on the other side of the living room.

"Hmph. That makes two of us." He sighed and fixed her with a crooked smile. "I figured you were getting

A Lover's Origin

tired of the pizza and Chinese Q was smuggling out here to us."

Tykira shrugged. "It wasn't so bad." She eased both hands into the back pockets of her jeans. She'd have probably been happy with peanut butter sandwiches if they were all he'd offered her.

Quay leaned against the counter and watched her more closely then. His gaze was unreadable as it scanned the length of her. Then, before his stare grew too telling, he looked away. "How 'bout a salad?" He turned for the fridge.

"Why'd you bring me here, Quay?"

He stopped his phony search for veggies and stood inside the open door of the refrigerator before turning towards her once again.

"Not that I'm complaining," she sounded rushed, "just that...we've never been... alone. Not even on those two pitiful dates we had if... you could call them dates. I guess I- I just thought that..." she trailed away when he suddenly bounded toward her.

Quay stopped short just before her. Tugging on the hem of her peach capped-sleeved blouse he brought her closer. Whatever questions Ty had rumbling about in her head, ceased when he put his hands on her. They'd been there in or around that cottage for over three days and he hadn't touched her once. It occurred to her then that he had never touched her.

Quay waited for some sign, some omen to stop him, to make him reconsider handling things this way. Signs and omens weren't necessary. This would happen and he'd deal with the consequences later. Her wide, expressive doe-

A Lover's Origin

shaped eyes studied his face with something so intense, he couldn't describe it. When she bit her bottom lip, he quit denying himself.

She moaned, becoming an eager participant in the kiss the second his mouth collided with hers. Desperately, she clung to the neckline of the lightweight Falcons sweatshirt he wore. Her fingers curved into the collar, she stood on her toes as they kissed and couldn't resist the feeling of being protected. She'd never been a tiny girl, but snuggled against him then, he made her feel small-diminutive.

Quay had expected *some* resistance on her part. There was none and it sent him half out of his mind. He knew she was a virgin- he had no proof of it but he knew. He'd have to remind himself of that often. The last thing he wanted was to hurt her- any more than he had to. He'd go slow when it mattered, he told himself and felt the buttons pop on her blouse when he yanked it open.

Her gasp filled the tiny confines of the kitchen but she showed no signs of resistance. She arched her breast into his palm when his hand cupped her there. She chanted his name as his tongue thrusted inside her mouth. She steeled herself against begging him to lay her down. Her head bumped the wall beneath the force of his kiss and she welcomed it. Her body jerked slightly when his hand delved inside the white lace of her bra and his thumb brushed a virgin nipple. Meanwhile, his other hand cupped the area where proof of her virginity rested beneath her jeans. Brazenly, she ground down against his hand before squeezing her thighs tight around it.

A Lover's Origin

Quay hoisted her against him then and carried her through the small bright living room to the decadent bedroom beyond it. It was still early afternoon, yet the vividness of the day didn't penetrate the room. There were no windows there; the room was lit by lamps with rose blush shades that carried low wattage bulbs. The round bed was made with the same rose blush coverings. They felt blissful beneath Ty when he placed her there on her back. She'd had the bed to herself for the past three nights- it had never felt as incredible as it did at that very moment.

In seconds, her shirt and bra lay in a heap upon the floor. Quay settled himself between her thighs still confined in the dark denims she wore. He cupped her breasts and outlined their shape with the tip of his nose.

Tykira was at a loss with what to do with her own hands. She let them tangle in her hair and cried out softly into the room as he took a nipple into his mouth. The sensations he evoked were so foreign yet now; experiencing them, she'd never felt anything more right.

He kissed his way down to her bellybutton all the while undoing the zipper of her snug jeans. Strong fingers curved around the waistband and tugged the denims along with her panties down her hips and thighs.

"Shh…" he urged when she gasped his name and lifted her hips from the bed. His nose was nudging her sex. He inhaled her aroma and let himself be drugged by it.

Ty settled down but her heart pounded anew with the discovery of the sensations stemming from his nose and then…she cried out and raked her nails across his silky hair when she felt his tongue inside her.

A Lover's Origin

Ravenous for her then, Quay clutched her bottom; that was half in and half out of her jeans, and feasted. Her cries in response to what he was doing to her triggered a surge to the arrogance that rarely traveled too far below the surface of his personality. He didn't stop treating her until she'd orgasmed twice in rapid succession. He took off what remained of her clothes while she moaned and circled her hips on the memory of what he'd just done to her.

Tykira felt her pleasure renew itself when he covered her body with his. He was as naked as she was and the realization of what was in store had her elated and terrified. Her thoughts were otherwise occupied when he kissed her and she tasted her body on his tongue.

He broke the kiss and a tiny moan of disappointment escaped her throat. She bit her lip and watched in awe as he eased a condom down the length of his shaft. That terrified feeling reared its ugly head as she studied his build and prayed he would tear her apart.

"This won't be fun at first," he said, apparently reading her thoughts when he returned to cover her body with his.

Something emboldened her then and she moved up to instigate a kiss. A shudder ripped through Quay. Burrowing one hand in her glossy tresses and wrapping the other around her upper thigh, he prepared to take her.

A small scream gurgled in the back of her throat when she felt the intrusion. Instinctively, she tried to shrink back, her hands curved into fists against his chest. Quay captured them, wrapping one hand about both her wrists and keeping them trapped between their bodies as he deflowered her in one long, firm stroke.

A Lover's Origin

The pain was fierce, but fleeing and Ty moaned mere seconds after her scream had silenced. Her hips seemed to have a mind of their own. They moved in sync with his and the sensations evoked were far from uncomfortable. Every part of her felt awakened and sensual. In the distance, she heard Janet crooning the melody *"Funny How Time Flies"*. Ty prayed with all her heart that wasn't true. She wanted this... forever...

Quay let his head rest on her shoulder and ordered himself to go slow with her. Impossible. She was everything to him. She always had been and sex had never once come into the picture. Now... now the reality of losing her, losing *this* was too much for him to think on.

So he dismissed it, releasing her wrists and capturing both her thighs to open her wider for him. She tried to stifle her cries, but had little success. Quay raised his head to watch the emotions play out across her lovely dark face. The fact that her expressions and reactions were all due to what he was doing to her stimulated his ego and hormones simultaneously. He grunted then, surprised by the sudden loss of control as proof of his satisfaction flooded inside the condom. Thankfully, Tykira was equally affected as the onset of her third orgasm caused her body to convulse on a wave of erotic bliss.

***

"Mmm... why are you dressed?" Ty was asking, offering Quay a dazzling smile when she woke.

He barely returned the smile while rushing around the room shoving things into a backpack. "I need to get you home."

A Lover's Origin

"Now?" Ty closed her eyes and snuggled deeper into the bed where they'd spent the better part of the last three and a half days.

"Sunday morning. Everybody's at church. Best time to go."

The clipped tone of his words had Ty raising her head to study him curiously. "Are you okay?"

"Yeah Tyke, but we need to get a move on.'"

She tugged a lock of hair about her index finger and made no move to leave the bed. "Can we… one more time?"

Her use of the phrase 'one more time' had Quay cursing below his breath. "No time," he felt sick to his stomach. He slung the backpack across his shoulder and headed for the bedroom door. "I'm outside waiting for Q. When you get dressed, come on out."

Ty wouldn't acknowledge the voice that told her something was very wrong. She watched the doorway Quay had exited for almost three minutes and then slowly left the bed.

***

On Monday morning, Tykira had no choice but to acknowledge the voice that had been trying to tell her things were very wrong. The boy she'd spent the most intimate week of her life with, was heading down their high school corridor with another girl clinging to his arm.

Everyone knew Quay had a sometimes hot, sometimes cold relationship with Jahzara Frazier. Things looked pretty hot between them that morning as they strolled the hallway looking totally absorbed with one another. When Quay walked by without so much as a

A Lover's Origin

glance, Ty opened her mouth to call him out. Thankfully, she caught herself before she could do anything else to humiliate herself.

Yes, everyone knew Quay and Zara had an off and on thing. That alone should've given her pause, Ty thought while watching the couple share a throaty kiss. What kind of girl did that make her? To sleep with another girl's guy? Ty figured she was simply getting her just desserts. Somehow, this didn't feel *just*.

Quay finally gave her the benefit of his dark, probing stare. Nothing warm or loving lurked there. There was humor though, especially when he whispered something to Zara who looked Ty's way and burst into laughter.

***

Somehow, Ty managed to make it though the rest of the week without breaking into a hysterical fit. Of course, she'd had plenty of opportunities to do just that. Quay's weird mood had become cold and hurtful. She cried herself to sleep every night and woke up calling herself all sorts of fools for giving such an idiotic boy that kind of control over her.

Leaning heavily on her anger, Ty guessed it couldn't have come at a better time than when she arrived home one afternoon to find him standing in her living room.

He had the nerve to smile at her which fired Tykira's anger even more. Before she took note of the *left* dimple and *gray* eyes, she'd hauled off and slapped him.

"Tykira what the-?!" Quest raised his hand defensively seconds after the blow landed on his cheek.

A Lover's Origin

"Oh God!" Ty covered her mouth with both hands, eyes stretched wide when she realized what she'd done. "What are you doing here?!"

"Came to get some papers for my dad," Quest risked a quick glance across his shoulder. "Your mom's upstairs."

Ty rolled her eyes. "I'm sorry," she pulled the barrette from her ponytail as she flopped down on the couch.

"What's up?" Quest took the armchair flanking the couch.

"Did you know?" She didn't care if he saw the water sparkling in her gaze. "Did you know he was gonna do that? Take me to that cottage and…"

The soft gray of Quest's stare simmered to black. "What'd he do?"

"Everything. Everything I always wanted or *thought* I did." She buried her face in her hands. "Then on Monday morning he acts like I don't exist and that Zara Frazier is suddenly the love of his life…again."

"Idiot…" Quest massaged his jaw. "Why-?"

"I have no clue," she shrugged. "I thought you would."

"I'll find out." He smoothed hand over fist. "You can bet I'll find out."

***

Tykira did a double take toward the wall clock in fifth period science when she saw Quaysar walking through the door. There were at least four minutes left before the start of class. Quay Ramsey never arrived until at least four minutes *after* the start of class.

A Lover's Origin

"Ty-"

"Oh? So you *do* remember my name?" She snapped when he was standing next to her lab table.

Quay smoothed his hand across the table's black surface and accepted the verbal slam. "I wanted to apologize."

She managed a smirk. "A Ramsey apologizing? Call the papers. This is a first."

"Ty please let me say this."

"Why? When I already know. You were horny, Zara wasn't around, so any old piece of ass would do."

"No Ty," he practically sighed the words. His hand curved into a fist.

Tykira wouldn't acknowledge what she saw in his eyes as regret. "Go away Quay. I'm sure Zara's looking for you. Sure you've got lots more laughing to do over me."

Quay ground down hard on his jaw before sitting down next to her. "Ty, me and Zara... you're too good for me, Ty."

She laughed quick- unamused.

"Girls like Zara- she's more my type, my speed." He rambled on while he had the nerve to get it all said. "I shouldn't have taken you out there, kept you there like that." He shrugged. "I was only thinking about what I wanted. What I didn't want anybody else to have until I- until I had my turn."

Tykira bristled, going cold beneath the aqua blue ruffled blouse she wore. Her hatred for him then, mingled with anger at herself for letting him fool her so totally, so easily for an entire week- as long as she'd known him.

A Lover's Origin

"You're a piece of shit Quay and you're right." She stood. "I *am* too good for you- stupid me for not seeing that before I let you inside me." She pulled her book bag from the table. "I have something for you. Gave it to Quest by mistake." With those words, she slapped him full and hard just as Zara arrived along with several of their classmates.

The group shared a laugh at Quay's expense while Ty ran from the room.

***

"Jesus Q!" Quay hissed when he arrived home from school that day and found his brother waiting patiently in his bedroom. "What's up?" He slammed his backpack to the clothes- littered armchair near the closet.

Quest didn't answer and it didn't take Quay long to figure why he was there.

"You talked to Ty?"

"What'd you do?" Quest's voice was little more than a whisper.

"If you talked to her, then you already know." Quay dropped to the bed and laid back.

Quest shook his head. "Why would you do that? The truth please and not the bullshit reason you gave her."

Quay slanted his twin a deadly, dark look. "Stay out of this, Q."

"Screw that. You put me in it when you asked me to take y'all out there. Why would you do this to her? You've been in love with the girl since the first time she came over here to play with us."

"Did you ever think maybe that's why I did it, Q? *Because* I love her?"

A Lover's Origin

Quest chuckled. "Now's not the time for you to try getting deep. Stick to what you're good at and tell it to me simple."

"If she hangs around me, she'll end up like the other ones and I can't have that happen. Not to her, Q."

"What the hell are you talkin' about?"

Quay pushed off the bed and scowled at Quest. "Have you already forgotten about the other girls who've gone missing?"

Realization dawned on Quest's handsome dark chocolate face and he threw his head back to laugh. He leaned forward then, cradling his head in his hands. "Not this shit again…"

"I know it's all connected, Q. I know it."

"And that's worth making her hate you?"

"Damn skippy, it is."

"And when all this shit is settled and you find out it had nothin' to do with your conceited ass, then what?"

Quay shook off the uncertainty his brother's words evoked. "I'll make it up to her if that day ever comes."

"And you're so sure she'll forgive you?"

Quay laid back down on the bed again. "Whether she does or not- at least she'll be safe…and alive."

Quest waved off the reasoning and stood. "I can't talk to you."

"Good."

"You're gonna regret this, you know?"

"Close the door on your way out." Quay reached over to pull a pillow over his face. When he heard the door click shut behind Quest, he shoved aside the pillow and burrowed the heels of his hands against his eyes.

A Lover's Origin

　　Somehow, someway she'd forgive him, trust him again- he'd see to it. She'd love him again, watch him the same incredible way she had when they were together those nights at the cottage.
　　He'd show Quest. He'd earn Ty's forgiveness but now was not the time to go looking for it. They'd be done with high school soon. With any luck, she'd head off far away and no one would ever suspect what she meant to him. She'd be far away and safe. That was what mattered.
　　Just then, that was *all* that mattered.

A Lover's Origin

Moses and Johari

"Why can't he come pick *you* up some time? God knows they've got enough cars." Johari Frazier blew a windblown tuft of red hair from her eyes and focused on the winding road she traveled in her burgundy Escort.

Zara Frazier didn't spare her sister a glance as she checked her flawless reflection in the tiny lighted mirror over the passenger seat.

"Quay gives me anything I want." She gave a flirty shake of her head, loving the way the curly hairstyle framed her face. "Least I can do is make myself available to him."

A Lover's Origin

"That's the problem with these guys, everything's too *available* for them."

"Jeez Jo, what the hell is your beef with the Ramseys?"

Johari's silver gaze narrowed as Damon and Catrina Ramsey's house appeared around the bend in the road. "They're too rich, too gorgeous and too sexy…"

"And those are bad things?"

Johari rolled her eyes. "I don't trust them."

"Look," Zara dropped her pink gloss stick into her purse and turned to face her sister. "Can't you cut 'em some slack? Our folks *do* work for them, remember?"

"Just…" Johari lost track of whatever she'd been about to say. A tall, dark and delicious looking specimen was leaving the house just as she pulled to a stop in the horseshoe driveway.

"Hmph," Zara followed the line of her sister's gaze. "Moses Ramsey." She waited for Johari to look her way. "In case you'd like to go and say hello."

"Just be careful." Jo said, just as her eyes locked with… Moses'.

"Don't wait up." Zara whispered while leaving the car.

Johari was way too focused on tall, dark and delicious to pay attention to her sister's parting words. Of course, he was a Ramsey- just her luck.

He'd opened the door to his Jeep but hadn't gotten inside. He stood there simply watching, silently offering her the chance to make herself *available* to him. Johari smarted then as though someone had hit her. She put the car in drive and sped back down the curving road.

A Lover's Origin

***

Days home alone held a special place in Johari's heart. They were the few times she could spend indulging in what was quickly becoming her favorite hobby: sunbathing. Her parents would have a fit if they knew she'd even thought of doing such a thing. Zara would probably laugh herself to death. Of course, none of them had the pale skin and freckles she felt she'd been cursed with. A nice turn in the sun gave what little melanin she possessed, the chance to do its thing.

Johari was on her way to the deck when the doorbell rang. *Zara*, she guessed with a quiet curse on her tongue. The girl was always forgetting her keys. So much for her favorite pastime, she mourned. Tucking the towel about her otherwise nude body, she flung open the front door expecting to see her sister.

"Moses Ramsey." He said as though appearing on her porch was nothing out of the ordinary.

Johari took a cautious step backward and tried to remember the warnings she'd given to her sister about the Ramseys. She couldn't remember any of them.

"My parents aren't home." She blurted the first things that came to mind and felt like a total idiot when he graced her with a devastating smile.

"That's good since I didn't come to see them."

Stop staring, dammit! She jerked to at the silent command. "I'm- I can't have company when they aren't here..." She looked down at her toes curling into the carpet.

Moses leaned back against one of the tall columns lining the porch. "Are you allowed to go out?" His voice

A Lover's Origin

sounded absent as his attention was more focused on the towel she clutched around her body.

"Well yes," she laughed shortly.

"Then I'll wait."

She laughed fully then. "I can't just... What makes you think I'd just go out with someone I don't even know."

He eased both hands into his jean pockets. "You'll come with me."

"Right," she leaned against the doorjamb. "Because you're a Ramsey."

Something soured in his pitch stare but he remained cool. "You'll come with me."

No doubt. She admitted to herself, already thinking of what to put on after the shower she wanted now instead of a turn in the sun. Every part of her was already tingling in anticipation of simply being in his presence- if only to look at him. She rolled her eyes, focusing on the carpet between her toes. How could she blame her reaction, though? The crop of glossy onyx hair that curled over his head, the long brows of that same glossy texture that slanted above the intense, vaguely unsettling dark eyes set deep and offering a dangerous element to his enticing molasses-toned features. Yes, every part of her tingled in anticipation of simply being in his presence.

"It's the only way you'll get me off your front porch, you know?"

She bristled despite the tingling. "Better my front porch than my living room". *Bedroom.*

He smirked as though approving of her countering remark. "Well that depends."

"On?"

A Lover's Origin

Moses shrugged, glancing briefly across his shoulder. "On whether your folks come back and wonder why you've got their bosses' son waiting out on the porch without so much as an invitation to come in?"

Johari's bristling turned into an outright scowl. At least the tingling had curbed… for a while. "I have to take a shower."

He pushed off the column. "I'll be back in twenty minutes."

"And if I'm not here?" She called, watching him stop halfway down the brick porch steps. She blinked, recognizing the look he turned to give her. It told her to stop trying to fool herself that she'd be anywhere other than right there when he returned.

"Why me?" Johari was asking before she settled into his car some twenty five minutes later.

Moses leaned on the passenger door he held open for her. "Why *not* you?"

"Because I'm not having sex with you."

"Not yet."

She felt her mouth thin into a grim line. Yet, as she watched him, she got the distinct feeling that he was intentionally goading her. The grim line eventually softened into a slight smile.

"Please?" His gaze slid toward the open door of the Jeep.

"You don't like me very much, do you?" Moses asked once he'd settled in behind the steering wheel.

"I don't even know you." Johari smoothed her hands across jean-clad thighs and stared straight ahead.

A Lover's Origin

He grinned and back out of the driveway. "But you know my family."

"Who doesn't?"

"So will you answer my question?" He stopped at the light leading out of the subdivision and faced her across the gear shift. His eyes were riveted on the uncommon shade of her bright hair and the silver stare that rivaled its brilliance.

"If I tell you the truth, will you have my parents fired?"

Moses laughed. "No!" He pressed the gas when the light changed. "Who knows? I may hate my family as much as you seem to."

Johari's mouth fell open. She had no response.

***

"Are we heading back?" Johari winced over the disappointment clinging to her voice when he took the turn leading to her side of town. They had driven all over town, taken in a movie and then a late lunch.

Moses glanced at the clock in the dash. "We've been gone almost four hours. Don't want your parents worrying- you being out with a Ramsey and all."

She laughed. "They'd probably throw me a party once I got back." She winced again. "Sorry."

He waved a hand. "Not a problem."

"Guess you never know whether girls are with you because you're rich or…"

"'Cause I'm so sweet?"

Her gaze faltered. She was going to say 'unbelievable to look at'. "That too," She told him.

A Lover's Origin

    Something changed in his expression and he took another turn. Johari silenced, not quite sure where they were headed then. Her bright eyes widened in playful surprise when he pulled to a stop before a local detective agency.

    Still, Moses offered no clues as to why they were there. Johari didn't question when he opened her door and escorted her inside The Simmons Agency & Bail Bonds.

    "Moses!"

    Johari smiled, immediately recognizing the owner Cooter Simmons. Cooter was a man not quite ready to let go of the few strands of hair he had left. She often heard her parents *discussing* their fellow choir member's penchant for combing the few miniscule tendrils across the ever widening scope of his balding head.

    Moses had already walked over to shake hands with the man and turned to wave Johari forward.

    "How are your parents, sugar?" Cooter was asking once he'd taken her hand.

    "They're good, thanks Mr. Simmons.'"

    Cooter nodded and clapped Moses' shoulder. "Staying long or just visiting?" He cast a speculative glance toward Johari.

    "Just visiting today, Mr. S. If it's okay I wanted to show Johari where I work."

    "Not a problem." Cooter Simmons threw a hand over his head and made his way over to the glass enclosed office at the back of the lobby.

    "Work?" Johari blurted.

    "Surprised?" He grinned.

    "Confused."

A Lover's Origin

Moses led her through the lobby. "Why? Because us Ramseys are lazy on top of being rich?"

"No." She watched him nod toward co-workers. "Because you're a Ramsey heir... why would you work here when you've got a place waiting for you there?"

"Maybe I don't want a place there."

Something in his tone told Johari her questions would only be met by vague answers. Instead she enjoyed the tour. She'd never seen the inside of a detective agency except for the ones on TV. The tour was a real treat, but it wasn't long before her pesky questions made their presence known again.

"What does Mr. Simmons let you do around here?" She asked, while watching a man across the room strap on a gun holster.

Moses leaned against a desk and folded his arms across the front of the Hawks T-shirt he wore. "Not much," he shrugged. "I'm mostly an errand boy for the bounty guys."

"Bounty guys?"

Moses nodded toward the man securing the gun holster. "Mr. Simmons does bail bonds- every now and again somebody skips. Those guys go to work- huntin' 'em down."

Johari's eyes widened.

Moses shrugged again. "Anyway, Mr. S lets me hang around, get 'em coffee, hunt files, shit like that."

"And you like this?" Johari fidgeted with the ruffled edge of her top and fixed him with a riveting stare.

"I learn a lot. These guys are a bunch of show offs, but good people and they love sharing stories."

A Lover's Origin

Johari scanned the busy room again. "Why would you be interested in this?"

Moses pushed off the desk. "Think I'd like to own a place like this one day. Command a group of bounty hunters."

She shivered. "Sounds like a grizzly job."

"Somebody's gotta do it." Moses grinned as they traveled beyond the offices.

"What's back here?" Johari asked when he led her into a room filled with file boxes.

Moses shut the door and the thud resounded in the confined space.

"Oh." Johari got the picture. Softly, she cleared her throat and took a step back only there was nothing to take a step back to. The boxes crowded her from behind. Moses' athletic frame blocked her front.

Her hands hung limp at her sides when his tongue slid into her mouth smooth and probing. She propped up a bit on her toes to more easily meet the kiss which had her moaning and sighing in unison. With an air of uncertainty she rested her hands against his chest, fingers curving slightly to feel more of the iron expanse of his chest.

Moses' touch was far bolder. He cupped Johari's bottom in his hands and tugged her up and into his groin. Neatly, he settled her against a stack of boxes and ground the proof of his need against her denim-clad sex. He broke the kiss, cupping her neck while angling it to expose the café au lait column to his mouth which grazed and suckled as it journeyed downward.

Johari bit her lip on the sounds coming from her throat and sounding louder along the way. He was incredibly strong and that alone was enough to make her moan. He supported her in his palms, flexing them around her bottom, grinding her against his arousal.

"Moses... mmm..." She meant to ask him to wait, but preferred to have him continue. The mounting pleasure was causing her to tremble and what followed was physically, emotionally and blissfully shattering.

He didn't cease grinding her against him when she climaxed. A smile of pure arrogance curved his sensually sculpted mouth.

"Mmm..." Johari's voice continued to waver as the orgasm ebbed. Orgasm? She was still fully clothed. This guys was dangerous and damned if she wasn't hooked.

Moses ceased his flexing about her derriere and waited for her odd, jerky movements to curb. He kissed her cheek and set her to her feet. Johari turned to make a play at fixing her clothes which were still in place. She could feel her cheeks burning and knew her face was beet red. She wouldn't make eye contact when he held open the file room door and barely lifted her head as they left the building.

He must have sensed her embarrassment for the ride back to her home was quiet. Johari wished the drive there would never end, mostly because she didn't know how she'd look him in the eye when it was time to say goodbye.

"Can I call you?" Moses was first to break the silence once he pulled to a stop before the Frazier residence.

"Why?" She blurted the word on a humorless laugh.

He smiled. "Why not?"

"I just made an idiot of myself."

"I didn't see it that way."

Her surprise kicked in. "Want to finish what you started, huh?"

He settled back against the driver's seat and appeared to be considering her question. "Guess you'd have to show me how to do that with a phone call."

Johari forbid herself to smile but knew he'd witnessed the twitching of her lips when she looked away.

"May I call you tonight, Johari?"

Her silver gaze lingered when she studied the sinful attractiveness of his face. Her expression was answer enough. "Good night Moses."

***

Two nights later, Moses had taken Johari out for dinner at Ariel's. The restaurant was located inside a small black-owned hotel called The Forman. Though both establishments had a great atmosphere and were nicely maintained, Johari was surprised that it would attract the attention of Ramsey caliber clientele. Moses laughed heartily when she shared her insights over dinner.

"My cousin Quay has had a back to school party here every year since just before we were freshmen." He shared proudly.

"Right," Johari focused on forking off another bite of the cheesy lasagna she'd ordered. "I've heard about those parties."

"You could've come, you know? Girls don't need an invitation to come."

"Hmph. How about to go?" She closed her eyes when the delicious pasta hit her tongue.

A Lover's Origin

"We don't force anyone to stay." A devilish smirk tilted his mouth. "We might...*encourage* the really fine ones to stick around a little longer though."

"So I've heard."

"Right...Zara's probably told you all about Quay's parties." Moses set the fork down next to his half eaten Ribeye and watched her. "Did I say something?"

Johari's head snapped up several seconds after she realized he'd asked a question. "What?"

"You've been kind of out of it since I picked you up. What's goin' on?"

She turned back to her lasagna. "Nothing."

He tapped his fingers to the tablecloth. "Did your parents give you grief about going out with me?"

"Are you kidding?" Johari tried to laugh, but failed. "It's Z. She didn't come home. I haven't seen her since I dropped her off at Quay's two days ago..."

"Did your folks call the cops?"

Johari nodded, absently twirling a lock of bright hair about her finger. "They called after the first day but the police said they couldn't do anything until she...until she's been missing longer."

Moses' probing ebony stare narrowed as he smoothed the back of his hand across his jaw. "Did Quay know anything?"

"They went out for lunch and then Zara hooked up with some of her friends. They said they'd gone to the mall and split up there. No one's seen her since."

Moses caught her hand before she could raise it to her mouth and bite her thumbnail. "Look, she's probably-"

A Lover's Origin

"No, no Moses. She's stayed out late before, but never all night and *never* for a whole weekend."

"Have you talked to all of her friends?"

Johari nodded. "Everybody we know of. God..." She pushed away her plate.

Moses reached for the sweater Johari had tossed over a vacant chair at the table. "I should take you home."

"No Moses please, I-" She clenched her outstretched hands into fists. "I don't want to go home- not yet."

"Alright." His smile was soft before he scanned the dining room for their waiter. He paid the check and they left soon after.

"I'm surprised my parents even noticed she was gone- they work so much..." She turned her face into Moses' chest while they cuddled on the bed. He'd gotten them a room inside The Forman. "I shouldn't have said that." She moaned.

He squeezed her closer. "You're upset."

"Moses what if she's-"

"Hey come on now. Don't think like that, okay?" He trailed his mouth against the fine hair smattering her temple.

The caress was only meant to soothe her, it did more. The fragrance of whatever she used to wash her hair had infatuated him since he'd first kissed her. The smell... a light mix of something fruity and floral triggered every sex hormone he owned. He'd been smoothing his hand up and down her back, a gesture also meant to soothe. It

A Lover's Origin

ventured beneath the light material of the aqua blue blouse she wore with a denim skirt.

Tiny moans radiated outward from Johari's throat. She kept her eyes closed while inhaling the incredible scent of the cologne clinging to her neck. The caresses he supplied to her body in an attempt to calm her, only aroused her. Unconsciously, she snuggled closer draping one thigh across his.

The affect on Moses was instant. His fingers curved briefly around the back strap of her bra and then he was pushing her to her back. Johari's skirt was fitted and wouldn't allow him to settle against her the way he wanted. The garment hit the floor moments later.

She whimpered when he removed her blouse at a slower pace. Once the buttons were undone, he traced her nose across the lush, light honey-toned cleavage. Johari arched her back, wanting more. She began to writhe against him, her panties doing little to shield the feel of the impressive length beneath his trousers.

A gush of air hit her skin. She hadn't even felt him pull off her bra and blouse. Her hips rotated against him with a greater sense of urgency. Moses left no part of her untouched, one flick of his wrist landed her panties on the floor next. He branded every part of her with his mouth and brought her to shattering climax twice before he removed a stitch of his own clothing.

"Moses..." She raked her fingers through the short glossy curls covering his head and then dragged them through her shoulder length reddish tresses. Overwrought with need, she couldn't be still.

A Lover's Origin

He held onto her hips firmly, indulging in a few glorious moments of suckling her nipples into rigid peaks. With Johari moving beneath him in such a yearning, naughty fashion he couldn't hold out long against his baser instincts.

Blindly, he reached for his jeans and wrenched a condom packet from the back pocket. He had the decency to appear uncertain when her silver stare snapped to his face.

"I um, I hoped we would..."

Johari smiled, cupping the back of his head and drawing him into her kiss.

She stiffened and a gurgled moan filled her throat when she felt the length and width of him filling her completely moments layer.

Moses kept his grip tight on her hips, preferring to direct her movements to his satisfaction- for the first time anyway. He'd wanted her since the moment he saw her. He honestly believed that he'd want her forever.

***

By the end of the week, talk in various Savannah circles revolved around the disappearance of yet another girl. No one wanted to admit that a pattern may have been developing. As all the disappearances involved young girls- young *black* girls. There was the possibility of a serial kidnapper or worse being on the loose. However, the fact that all the girls were of color could have implied the involvement of some racial motivation and no one wanted to imagine the ramifications of that.

"They sure she's... gone?"

A Lover's Origin

    Moses barely nodded in response to Quay's question. "Johari called me this morning- said the cops were all over the place."

    "Maybe she just took off for a few days." Quest said in a clearly skeptical tone.

    "She didn't take any of her stuff…" Moses focused on rubbing his hands one over the other. "It's like she just disappeared…"

    The twins exchanged meaningful looks. Their cousin noticed.

    Moses' pitch stare narrowed. "What?"

    Again, Quest and Quaysar looked toward each other.

    "Q?"

    "I broke up with Zara- it was the last time I saw her." Quay shared.

    "Was it the day I came over here?" Moses asked.

    The twins were already nodding.

    "Last Saturday." Quay supplied. "She um…" he left the sofa and began to pace his mother's sunroom. "She told me she was pregnant."

    Moses closed his eyes. "Jesus…"

    "She told me after I told her I wanted to break up- that the only reason I was with her was to make Ty mad…" Quay muttered something foul and slammed his fist against the back of the sofa.

    "Why would you do that?"

    "Shit Moses, you know the hell why! What's this now? Zara makes three of 'em, right? Or is it four now? I'm losin' count!"

    Quest left the sofa then to go soothe his brother.

A Lover's Origin

"I wasn't gonna let that shit touch Tykira." Quay vowed, glaring at his cousin from across Quest's shoulder. "I woulda said, done anything to get her the hell away from me."

Quest turned to Moses then too. "Quay thinks this is personal- somebody goin' after girls he's interested in."

"I don't *think* it, I *know* it." Quay grumbled from his leaning stance against a wall.

Quest was more interested in Moses' reaction just then. "What? Moses?" He pressed when Moses would only shake his head.

Quay stepped closer to where his cousin sat and waited for him to speak up too.

"I don't wanna talk about it right now, okay?"

"You know somethin'?" Quay guessed.

"I suspect something."

"Hell Mo, if you got somethin' here speak on it. Maybe the cops-"

"No Quay. Trust me, whatever I *suspect*... if it's got merit then the cops are the last folks who'll do anything about it."

Again, the twins exchanged meaningful glances. Quest nodded then, accepting Moses' opinions on behalf of himself and his brother.

***

"I shouldn't be here." Johari's voice was barely audible when she stood just inside the room Moses had booked at The Forman.

Moses closed the distance between them. He squeezed her shoulders, pulling her back against him and leaning down to press his cheek next to hers.

A Lover's Origin

"God knows what could be happening to my sister and I'm here-"

"Shh... this isn't your fault. She wouldn't want you thinking that."

"Is she able to *think* at all? Moses what if she's..." Johari wouldn't finish the troubling sentence. Losing control then, she turned and cried heavily against his chest.

"Let me take care of you Jo..." he rocked her slow. Eventually, the tears; soaking the front of his sweatshirt, began to ebb.

Moses tightened his hold around her body and sighed his content. He could tell that the embrace was working its calming powers upon Johari. It worked equally well for him. As long as he held onto her, he could forget the suspicions filling his mind. For a while, at least.

A Lover's Origin

Carlos and Dena

Dena Ramsey bit her lip on the scream that was seconds away from being released into the night air. She'd been doing a good enough job of maintaining her quiet since she'd been set atop the hood of the black Ford truck and... according to her boyfriend, dealt with.

Her hands splayed against the windshield allowing her to add more force to the rhythm of her hips.

"Are you losing respect for me?" Her voice was a whisper as she shifted the rotation of her ride.

Carlos McPhereson winced. The pleasure provided by the slender dark lovely above him made it impossible to think of any words or how to relay them for that matter.

A Lover's Origin

"Hmm?" Dena persisted having a good idea as to the affect she had on the gorgeous honey toned male beneath her.

Carlos grasped a fist full of the flaring vibrant colored skirt Dena wore for their date that evening. His other hand clutched an ample portion of her bare bottom, loving the way the flesh flexed against his palm when she glided up and down the length of him.

"Carlos?"

"Hell yeah," he finally responded to her question, "losing more and more respect for you every minute."

Her laughter filled the air then. Carlos let go of her skirt and clutched her bottom in his large grasp. She lost strength in her hands and everyplace else, for that matter. Carlos took over, maneuvering her body to his satisfaction as he claimed her with a savage beauty atop the hood of his truck.

Dena raked her nails across the chiseled expanse of his massive chest visible through the opening of his shirt. She marveled over the power rippling from his body. The way he handled her- the sight of him alone was enough to get her wet and keep her that way.

He hissed a curse, his ruggedly handsome face a picture of torture and elation when he felt her coming against him. He wouldn't allow her to collapse against his chest until his own climax followed some time later.

"I like the way you say goodbye." Carlos' deep voice was little more than a growl.

Dena tried to maintain her smile and cuddled closer where they lay atop the hood of the truck following their

A Lover's Origin

delicious encounter moments earlier. "I wish I didn't have to say goodbye." She admitted. "Daddy's acting so weird about this trip."

"You mean weirder than he usually acts?" Carlos said and braced himself for the punch she planted to his abs.

"I don't think it's really my dad who's givin' me the creeps about it, but uncle Marc."

Carlos' easy expression tightened when he felt Dena shiver against him. "What about your uncle Marc?" He gave a tug to one of the glossy black spiral curls that framed her face.

"This trip was *his* idea and then I can't get daddy to tell me a thing about it."

"You talk to your mom?"

"Hmph." Dena focused on the pattern her thumbnail traced around one of his taut pectorals. "She doesn't care. It's the chance to schmooze with somebody's rich son so… she's all for it."

"Rich sons, huh?" Carlos' green eyes narrowed and he tightened his grip playfully about Dena's waist.

She giggled. "Trust me, no one gets any father than the sound of my voice."

"Damn straight," he growled.

The couple dissolved into laughter before the sweet act of kissing resumed.

***

"You're going to have the time of your life, sweetness. You'll meet lots of girls and make lots of new friends. So many girls here are right around your age."

A Lover's Origin

Houston Ramsey went on as he and his daughter followed the porter who had their bags.

"What *is* this place, daddy?" Dena saw her father tense just as she looked away from the high ceilings and chandeliers filling the foyer. She couldn't be sure if they were inside a hotel or someone's mansion.

"That porter will take you on to your room, sugar." Marcus Ramsey interrupted, closing his hand over Houston's arm to prevent him from moving on. "Your daddy and me got some business to take care of so we'll see you later on, alright?"

Dena didn't bother to mask the suspicion in her dark eyes as she regarded her uncle. She accepted her father's encouraging smile for what it was though and followed the porter who waited patiently.

Marcus Ramsey sent his brother a guarded look, and then watched his niece walk on until she was out of sight.

Her father was right, Dena noted as she followed the fast moving porter. There were girls everywhere laughing, running, screaming like wild and free women. Some though, looked as lost as she did. They were of all nationalities. Most were her age, though she could have sworn she saw others who looked much younger. The porter whisked her down another corridor before she could get a better look at them though.

Dena promised herself that once the porter left, she'd try finding someone who could tell her where she was and what the hell was going on.

***

A Lover's Origin

The odd collection of guests gathered later in a gargantuan dining room. Dena had been able to find out the place was a mansion- a palatial one, but not a hotel as she'd assumed earlier. Unfortunately, she'd been able to discover little else. The arrangement of the dining room had guests seated along one of four extremely long tables which curved fancily at either end. Electric candles lined the middle of each table that; combined with the chandeliers overhead, gave the room an ethereal golden tint.

There were so many girls, Dena noted and not with a sense of contentment. There were *too* many girls dressed in clothing more appropriate for women much older. She took note of her own prom-like attire and wondered why her father had insisted she pack such formal clothing. Stranger still, there were no boys, but plenty of men. It was a mystery as to who they were and why they were seated amongst the slew of chattering young women. Dena hadn't seen her father or her uncle since arriving that afternoon. Instead of feeling frightened, she felt suspicious.

"Don't you like the food?"

Dena jumped at the sound of the voice so close to her ear. Her fork slid from her fingers to clatter against the side of her plate. She turned to the girl who had spoken.

"It's not so weird once you get used to it." The girl's eyes sparkled deep and black as she glanced toward her own half eaten food.

Dena gave a one shoulder shrug. "I've had salmon before. Pretty fancy for a bunch of teenagers," She scanned the room again.

The young woman scanned the room as well. "I think it's supposed to make us feel elegant."

"What is this place?" Dena blurted and followed the girl's gaze toward another young woman who was being fed ice cream by a man.

"Paradise... for some," the girl said.

Dena's mouth was hanging open.

"Evangela Leer." The girl introduced herself.

"Dena... Dena Ramsey."

Evangela nodded and then reached for two saucers from the tray of a passing waiter. "Try the mousse, it's really good."

"What is this place, Evangela?"

"Later okay?" Some of the vibrancy dimmed on Evangela's dark pretty face as she stirred a spoon in the chocolate dessert.

Dena turned in her chair. "Later when?"

"Just later, okay?" Evangela's voice was almost a hiss then. She looked around quickly and then sent Dena a weak smile. "After, alright?"

Something told Dena she'd get nothing else out of Evangela Leer. Nothing that made sense, anyway. Sighing, she turned her focus to the mousse. It really was quite good.

***

Dena rolled her eyes and turned away from her room door the following afternoon when Evangela visited. Barefoot, Dena padded across the plush peach-colored carpeting to resume her place along the heavily cushioned window seat.

"You knew what they were gonna do, didn't you?" Dena stared past the curtains but didn't really see the beauty that was the rear lawn of the house.

A Lover's Origin

"Why didn't you tell me?" Dena asked, glaring at Evangela who stood a few feet away. "Why didn't you-"

"Why? So you could what?" Evangela's pleasant expression took on a dark sheen. "What? Ruin what we have here?"

"And what is that?" Dena swung her legs from the seat.

Evangela stepped back to regard her with a smirk. "What do you think?"

"What I think is disgusting."

"In your opinion."

"In *any* opinion! If the police knew-"

"What makes you think they don't?!" Evangela closed the distance between them and clutched handfuls of Dena's robe when she knelt before her. "What makes you think the most powerful men in the most powerful positions in the most powerful countries in the world, don't know?"

Dena's lashes fluttered and she bowed her head low over her chest. "What could they want with my…" her arms curved about her belly.

Evangela shrugged, looking down towards her own waist then. "Who knows… probably trying to create something with our ovaries…almost as many scientists around here as perverts."

"Bitch!" Dena pushed Evangela away. "You're as sick as they are for letting them get away with this. I've seen girls here who can't be more than twelve!"

"Yeah…" Evangela tucked a lock of her bobbed hair behind an ear. "I think they keep the younger ones someplace else."

A Lover's Origin

  Dena pushed off the window seat and ran to the bathroom. There, she fell to her knees before the toilet and vomited.
  Evangela came over to lean against the doorjamb. She smiled, watching as Dena dry-heaved into the bowl. "Don't worry. Your daddy will take you back to your fairy tale life soon. But you're one of us now and that won't ever change."
  Evangela sauntered over to where Dena still hovered on the floor. She pulled the hair back from Dena's temple and planted a soft kiss there. "We'll always be connected. One day you'll understand what that means." She said and then left Dena alone.

***

  She knew he'd come to see her sooner or later. Her excuses to him over the phone for the last week and a half, had grown flimsier and flimsier. But she had to talk to him. She had to tell him something. She owed him that much at least.

  Carlos pulled her into a kiss the second she closed the door behind him in the foyer. His kiss was deep, passionate, punishing. For a while, Dena lost herself in the delight of it. She took herself back to before her life had been turned inside out. Eagerly, she drove her tongue against his loving the feel of his big, hard frame and how secure she felt against it.
  "Why are you keeping me away? Why won't you talk to me?" He fired the questions when she suddenly broke the kiss. "Dena what-"
  "I can't see you anymore, Carlos."

A Lover's Origin

He took a step back. "Just so I'm clear," he laughed shortly and scratched at the soft hair curling along his temple. "I haven't seen you since that night on top of my truck, right?"

Dena cleared her throat on the moan that the memory stirred. "This isn't about you."

"Right," he raked the length of her body with the emerald intensity of his gaze. "My girlfriend tells me she can't see me anymore and it's not *about* me? Then what's it about?" He folded his arms across his chest. "Or *who*?"

Dena went cold beneath her maroon sweater. "What do you mean?"

"Come on De," he brushed past her. "At least be honest enough to tell me you met somebody on that fuckin' ritzy ass trip of yours."

"No." Her voice was faint as she shook her head. "Carlos please," she followed him across the foyer when he waved off her denial. "It's just better if you're not around me. Me or my family."

"Right, right…" he massaged both hands to the back of his neck and grimaced as if he'd suddenly remembered. "I keep forgetting that I don't come from your *world*."

"Carlos…" She couldn't say more.

"So that's it?" He shook his head. "All this time, all that- that's happened and you just end it like this?" He swiped an empty vase from its stand as he walked past.

"It's better this way."

"What way?! You won't even tell me what the fuck is goin' on De!"

A Lover's Origin

Dena gathered what little strength she had and went to the front door. She pulled it open. "You need to go now Carlos."

He watched her as though she were a stranger. Clearly there was more to be said, but Carlos knew it was useless. She was gone- lost wherever her father had taken her. Something had happened there that changed her. Until she shared it, they didn't stand a chance. Carlos knew she wouldn't be up for sharing anytime soon.

Dena just managed to shut the door when he walked out. The strength left her legs and she fell to the floor while clinging to the doorknob. She cried until she was spent and then cleaned up the shards of the broken vase and returned to her bedroom before anyone got home.

Carlos would hate her forever, but that was okay. She didn't like herself much then either.

A Lover's Origin

Smoak and Sabra

The look on his face alone should have told her it was a mistake to come there. Of course she'd never been very good at listening to what that wise inner voice usually told her.

"Will you let me explain?" Sabra Ramsey's maple brown eyes were wide with uncertainty and in hopes of staving off the tears behind them.

"Explanation's required only if there's confusion. No confusing what I saw." Smoak Tesano's rich deep voice possessed a hushed tone.

Sabra knew he was livid. His voice only went quiet that way when he was angry-which was most of the time.

A Lover's Origin

Thankfully, she'd never had the emotion directed at her. Hmph, that was all changed now.

"Would you please let me explain anyway?" Slowly, she moved forward wringing her hands and wishing he'd turn around so that she could see if his expression was softening.

Of course her present view of him was nothing to complain about. He had an intense dislike for wearing clothes when he was at home alone. Sabra wondered if he'd checked the privacy window before opening his apartment door in the buff. His massive muscular frame was drenched in the most beautiful blackberry tone. Flawless, chiseled... perfect. What man, with a body like that would want to cover it?

Sabra's expression masked none of the arousal his body stirred. When Smoak turned and caught her staring, he smirked and waited for her gaze to meet his.

"Did you come here to talk or to stare?"

Her eyes had been focused below his waist, her mouth gone dry from the most appealing part of his anatomy. Somehow, she managed to bring herself back into the situation at hand.

"You have to understand..." she moved closer. "What you saw- with me and Brogue. We were drunk and..." She winced, the *explanation* sounded pathetic even to her.

Smoak trailed the back of his hand along the side of his face which was even more magnificent-looking than his body. "So you're here expecting me to understand that you let him fuck you because you were drunk?"

"I don't mean it that way- just... I didn't mean it."

A Lover's Origin

He rolled his eyes. "Get out."

"Smoak please," she followed him out of the living room and down the short corridor. "I didn't mean to sleep with him-"

"Who said anything about you sleeping with him?" He stopped suddenly and turned. "I mean, that *was* my cousin in your bed with his dick inside you, right?"

She couldn't have hurt more than if he'd slapped her. "I never intended for it to go that far." She didn't care about the tears streaming from her eyes then. "I was already home and... drinking and he- he just came over and-"

"Came again?" Smoak finished and headed on down the hall.

Sabra lost her temper then and charged after him. "Screw you!"

"Yeah, that's what I had in mind when I showed up at your place." He went into the apartment's second bedroom which he used for a study/lab.

"You had screwing in mind?" Sabra folded her arms over her breasts, barely concealed beneath the deep purple halter she wore. "You had screwing in mind," she spoke as though talking to herself. "I find that hard to believe when you're always stuck up in this office of yours working!"

"Maybe you should try it more often." He browsed through a heavy book he'd pulled off a shelf. "That's what college is for, right?"

"Spare me the bullshit, please!" She threw her hand up and swiped some papers from a chair. "There is more to college than working all the damn time. You never want to have any fun and you ridicule *me* for wanting to have any!"

A Lover's Origin

Smoak's thick, silky brows rose a few notches above his charcoal gaze. "Ridicule? That's a big word for you, isn't it?"

"You're an ass."

"And you're spoiled." He slammed down the book and faced her. "Everything always handed to you and your cousins on a silver platter."

"Look who's talkin'! Your family has more money than God!"

Smoak brushed past her on his way out of the room. "There's a difference between having it and having access to it." He rested back against the doorway leading to his bedroom. "Maybe it's not the money at all with Brogue, though?" He shrugged. "Maybe it's a skin tone thing."

Sabra curled all ten fingers through her hair and stifled a scream. "Not this shit again! I'm so sick of this racial crap you've got with your family. Would you be this upset if I'd fucked around on you with a black guy instead of a white one?!"

He made a move toward her. Sabra backed off, swallowing over the lump of emotion that had swelled in her throat.

"Get out of here, Sabra."

"Can't you just accept that it happened and it's over?" She followed him across the spacious, neat bedroom not willing to lose him. "What happened didn't mean anything- nothing! I don't have any feelings for Brogue and I never will!"

"Thought you guys were friends?"

She slammed a palm to her fist. "You know what I mean. We were drunk."

A Lover's Origin

"Right. That makes it all better, I guess?" He massaged the rugged curve of his jaw.

"No." She couldn't read the look on his dark, beautifully crafted face. "It's just the reason it happened Smoak. The *only* reason."

"Mmm..." He appeared to consider her words and then left the bedroom.

Sabra followed. The voice of wisdom told her to head for the front door instead. Remaining true to form though, she didn't listen. Smoak had gone into the kitchen where he proceeded to slam through a few cabinets until he found a bottle half full of gin. Again, Sabra swallowed around that lump of emotion in her throat and watched him chug down an obscene amount.

"Smoak..." She whispered, unconsciously backing away when he slammed the bottle down and came after her.

It didn't take much for him to catch her. She could have moved lightning fast and he'd have had her. Her heart thudded wickedly in her chest and she could barely hear anything above it in her ears.

She braced her hand against his bare chest when he grabbed her arms. Part of her was scared witless. Part of her was paralyzed by some other emotion she couldn't identify. It didn't even occur to her to fight him.

"Don't," she managed when his fingers curled into the square bodice of her halter.

Smoak hesitated but a split second before tearing the material clear off her back. The rest of her clothing hit the floor in a rapid fashion until she was as bare as he was.

"Smoak..." she wilted when he weighed one breast while brushing the sensitive nub of her clit with the other.

A Lover's Origin

When his middle finger thrust high and rotated inside her, she smothered a trembling moan. "You don't want to do this." She managed.

His hold on her breast firmed and he drew her closer. "But I'm drunk, remember? I can do whatever I want, right?"

Her heart was in her throat. She couldn't speak. It didn't matter. Her mouth was otherwise occupied a moment later. The voice of wisdom was literally screaming at her then. *Fight him and go*, it urged warning her against being a slave to something as fleeting as desire. Hadn't desire brought enough trouble to her door?

Sabra drove her tongue against his, effectively silencing the cautions. She grazed her nails across the awesome power of his chest and shuddered when her nipples brushed the unyielding expanse of it.

Smoak wasn't in the mood for tenderness though. In one deft move, he jerked her high against him, slipping his arms beneath her so that her legs were hooked over his forearms. She grunted when he started taking her without mercy in the middle of his living room.

"No," she moaned, not to resist but to relay her disappointment when he eventually slowed the drives inside her. She knew this was a punishment. It felt like anything but that.

Smoak averted his face when she would have kissed him. He didn't want her sweetness. He wanted to hurt her the way she'd hurt him. It would have been a helluva lot easier if he didn't love her so.

A Lover's Origin

She moaned without shame, nuzzling his ear and smoothing her fingers across the glossy, blue-black crop of hair covering his head.

Smoak moved then, taking her back to the bedroom. He tossed her to the bed and only watched her for a few seconds before following her down.

Instinctively, Sabra backed away and was dragged back to the middle of the bed when he caught her ankle. Her hair flew into her face when he flipped her to her stomach and took her from behind.

Sabra clutched the covers and met his heated thrusts with her own brand of intensity. Her movements lost some of their steam when she climaxed.

Smoak could feel her saturating the length of his shaft and almost melted on top of her. He was but a hair's breadth from reaching his own level of satisfaction but he wanted to... *punish* her a little more.

She was practically out of breath and prepared to beg for a break when he withdrew and covered her with his wide frame. He wound his arms about her waist.

The sounds rising from Sabra's throat then had a tortured undertone. Smoak alternated between fingering her and stroking her labia with his thumbs. She buried her face in the tangled covers and ground her bottom into his still throbbing sex.

Smoak didn't make her wait long. Curving his hands about her thighs, he spread her to his preference and had her again. Her sobs were muffled into the pillows...

Hours later, Sabra was waking from another light nap. Smoak had allowed her a few during the extent of her

A Lover's Origin

visit that afternoon. She took a moment to collect herself and then began to ease out of the bed.

"Goin' somewhere?" He asked upon returning to the room.

Sabra settled back against the headboard, drawing the sheets to her neck.

"Thought this was your favorite place?"

She closed her eyes. "Smoak-"

"More?" He didn't wait for an answer but threw the sheet to the floor with the rest of the covers.

Sabra had lost track of how many times she'd found herself in the middle of his bed that day. "You don't have to do this." She told him.

Smoak settled himself against her. "But I'm drunk, remember? I've got a damn good reason for doing this."

Sabra opened her mouth when she felt him. There was no sound from her throat, but her pleasure went without saying. He wouldn't let her move. His grip; flexing along the thick line of her thighs, was strong as a vice while he enjoyed her.

She felt depleted and in the most delicious way. Her intimate walls were bruised and thoroughly used. Her voice returned, but she could only use it to grunt in sync to his body pummeling hers.

"You can go." Smoak grabbed the sheet from the floor and tossed it over Sabra when he left the bed.

The sheet felt freezing cold against her heated skin. She wrapped it around her and grimaced while pushing up in the bed.

A Lover's Origin

"Tell my cousin I'm sorry for not using a condom." He kept his back toward her yet tilted his head toward the bathroom. "You might want to clean up first before you crawl back in the sack with him. Sure he won't appreciate *coming* after me of all people."

Sabra screamed, her temper unleashed and ready to land on him. She threw herself against his back, clawing at its flawless dark width. "I hate you! You mixed-race son of a bitch!"

As if she were an annoying gnat, Smoak slung her off him. When she landed on the bed, he followed and clutched his hand about her neck.

"I'm a mixed raced son of a bitch and you're a ho who can't get enough." He sneered, speaking the words close to her ear. "I practically raped you and you moaned the whole time. Now get your shit before I forget about letting you up out of here."

The fire lighting Sabra's temper was doused as quickly as it had been ignited. With a death grip on the sheet, she pulled herself from the bed. Whatever dignity she had was gone and she didn't care if he heard her crying like an infant while she gathered her things. She went to the living room to dress and left soon after.

Alone, Smoak felt the need to inflict more pain and bolted out to the living room with intentions of trashing it. He got no farther than the doorway where he fell to his knees, pressing the heels of his hands against his eyes. The pressure of tears behind them came as no surprise. He wouldn't give into them though. Giving in to them was a call for mercy, pity. He deserved none of that after what he'd done. Sure she'd *hurt* him, but had her punishment fit

A Lover's Origin

the crime? Moreover, was the real issue not what she'd done but *who* she'd done it with? If he deserved anything, it was her hate. He was sure she carried bucket loads of it for him now.

***

Kenny Kenny was a popular dance club with San Diego's college crowd-especially its black college crowd. Started by cousins Kenneth Anderson and Kenneth Geralds, the place not only boasted the best DJs, food and atmosphere but a long list of the hottest R&B and Hip Hop acts of the day.

It was also one of Sabra Ramsey's favorite places. At the moment, it was her *only* favorite place. The Kennys; like most of the guys who knew her or knew of her, were smitten. The Kennys however were *smitten* enough to furnish her with an unending tab at their bar. That night, Sabra decided to show her appreciation. She'd been one of the first past the doors when the club opened hours earlier. At the onset of the fifth hour, her unending tab was beginning to show signs of wear and tear.

Quest Ramsey had lost interest in whatever idle (idiotic) chatter his dates rattled on with. Sheena Welch and Audrey Meeks didn't mind that he had zoned out of the conversation. He relaxed on the sofa with his eyes closed and feet propped to the glass table before them. A call for a date with Quest Ramsey was a coup for any girl even if she had to share him. Audrey and Sheena were as content as two cats over a bowl of cream.

"Quest?" Sheena called, softly brushing her fingertips along the side of his smooth molasses-toned

A Lover's Origin

cheek. "Quest?" She nudged his shoulder and smiled up at Kenny Anderson who had just approached them.

"Sorry man," Kenny glanced toward the two adoring girls who sat on either side of his friend. "Can I have a sec?"

Audrey and Sheena pouted as their *date* left without explanation or a word of farewell.

"It's Sabra, man." Kenny spoke close to Quest's ear when they stood inside one of the corridors leading toward the offices.

"Where is she?" Quest's easy demeanor had sharpened.

Kenny nodded toward the bar. "She can hardly sit up, man. Didn't think y'all would want anybody seein' her like that."

"Find my brother." Quest told Kenny and headed for the bar.

Smoak cast an agitated look toward his wristwatch and cursed Pike for deserting him at their table. He'd only taken his brother up on the offer to go out to get him off his back. Word of the dramatic Tesano/Ramsey break up had spread among the black student network like an aggressive cancer. Pike wouldn't let his younger brother hide out in his apartment to lick his wounds over Sabra. Smoak wasn't easily bullied, but that night he made it pathetically simple for his brother to do it. Now, he sat alone and regretted his decision. His expression was so shadowed and harsh, the scores of girls who considered approaching him, thought twice.

A Lover's Origin

Muttering one last curse, Smoak stood and pulled out money for the wings and beer they'd ordered. He was slipping his wallet back into his jeans when his pitch stare scanned the bar... and he saw Sabra.

"Mmm... Smoak?" Sabra's smile was lazy. Her eyes were closed.

"No babydoll, it's Q." Quest leaned down to drape her arm across his shoulder.

The serene smile Sabra wore began to tremble. "Why'd he do me that way Q? Why?"

"I don't know, babe. Here, hold onto me." Quest eased an arm below her knees and pulled her against his chest.

"I went to tell him..." Sabra frowned on the wave of dizziness that claimed her and she turned her face into Quest's neck. "I went to tell him why and he- he wouldn't let me... explain..."

"I know babe, I know." Quest nodded toward the bar when he saw Quay approaching.

"What's the damage, Tiny?" Quay was pulling bills from his wallet.

The tall, rotund Puerto Rican behind the bar waved off the money. "Just take care of her." His voice and dark eyes filled with concern over Sabra.

Quay grimaced toward his intoxicated cousin. "We'll try." He pulled out several bills and stuffed them into Tiny's tip jar. "Thanks man."

"Sabra!" Smoak was barreling toward the bar. He came to a sudden halt when Quay blocked his path. "Is she alright?"

A Lover's Origin

Quest spared Smoak a half-second glare and then headed for the exit with Sabra in his arms. Quay decided on a response with a little more kick and let his fist connect with Smoak's jaw.

"Come near her again and your gangsta family won't find out where we buried the body." Quay snatched Sabra's things from a barstool. "You can pass that on to the white boy too." He referred to Brogue Tesano.

The pain of the blow barely registered to Smoak. His eyes were still focused on Sabra being carried out the door.

***

"Fernando went to get something from his apartment. He'll be right back."

Despite his mood, Smoak had to smile at the warning Sabra blurted when she found him outside her door the following evening.

"Do you really think your cousins scare me, Sabe?"

She couldn't meet his gaze and stepped back to let him inside her apartment.

Smoak saw her debating on whether to shut the door. He took the decision out of her hands and leaned over to close it. "I promise not to touch you." He spoke close to her ear.

Sabra didn't know how to feel about that. Tugging on the tassels of her white hoody she went to stand in the middle of the living room.

"Are you okay?"

She thought she'd misheard him. "Am I...okay?"

A Lover's Origin

Smoak ran a hand across the blue-black crop of hair that capped his head. "I don't ever expect you to believe this. I *am* sorry."

Her heart lurched but she wouldn't acknowledge it. She fought against what it inspired within her. "It's like you said," she shrugged indifferently and went to sit on the sofa. "I moaned the whole time- I guess that proves you didn't do anything wrong."

"You can't mean that?" He closed his eyes in regret while massaging the bridge of his nose.

"Why are you here Smoak? To apologize?" She nodded and slapped her hands to her knees. "I accept."

"I won't hurt you like that again." He swallowed the bile that rose at the back of his throat. "I'll never touch you that way again."

"Promises, promises." Sabra muttered, though she was mortified to discover a part of her was disappointed by his words.

Smoak moved toward the sofa, but stopped short as though realizing he was moving closer to her. "We shouldn't see each other again."

Again, she shrugged. "I sort of figured that'd be the end result when you found me in bed with your cousin."

"That's not why, babe." He smirked when she studied him in disbelief. "You were right. It wasn't what you did but who you did it with." He turned away from her then. "What I feel for Brogue, for his side of our family…" he flashed her a half smile. "It's ugly and it'll get uglier before it gets better. I don't want you to…" he grunted at the taste of more bile souring his throat. "I don't want you

A Lover's Origin

knowing that part of me Sabra. I don't want you to know any *more* of that part of me."

Sabra pressed her hand to her mouth. She wanted to stop him. She wanted to tell him what happened didn't matter to her. It mattered to him though. It mattered to him too much for anything good to come from them being together ever again.

There wasn't much else to say. Sabra wouldn't look at him. Smoak took advantage of that to memorize every curve and nuance of her very beautiful toffee brown face.

Once he'd left, Sabra treated herself to a good cry and forbid herself to ever shed tears for him again. She knew that was a command she'd never obey. It would suffice for the time being, along with the tall bottle of Vodka she'd cracked the seal on before Smoak Tesano had come to deliver his goodbyes.

A Lover's Origin

Isak (Pike) and Sabella

"I mean, why couldn't they have given me a convertible or something?"

Sabella Ramsey smiled but didn't look away from the full length mirror she stood in front of. "Because you already have one?" She reminded her cousin.

Sabra shrugged. "You can never have too many convertibles."

Sabella decided against pinning up her hair. "You're crazy." She let the dark brown waves fall past her shoulders. "I'd take land over a car any day."

"Then I'll ask daddy and uncle West to give it to you and buy me a new convertible." Sabra flounced off the bed as though the plan was set in her mind.

A Lover's Origin

"Sabi what's the problem?" Sabella's temper was so hard to rouse, it could be argued that she didn't have one. Of course, it had always been easy for her cousin to locate.

"Are you forgetting the land is in Vegas? *Vegas.*" She glared through the mirror at Sabra.

"And are *you* forgetting I told you Smoak was gonna be there?" Agitated then, Sabra loosened and then retied the halter strap of the bathing suit she sported. "Uncle West said Smoak's grandfather just died and there's been a *rearranging* of things or some shit like that. Looks like Smoak's been given some property too and now I've got to go out there and sign *more* papers?" She rolled her eyes. "It all sounds funky to me."

"Sabi-"

"And don't you try tellin' me I'm overreacting!"

"Alright, I won't." Belle left the mirror to go hunt for a cover-up to the swimsuit she wore. "All I'm saying is property in Vegas is nothin' to sneeze at."

"Sneezing is *all* I'll be doin' out there." Sabra chose to whip her freshly flat-ironed hair into a ponytail. "What the hell am I suppose to do out in the desert? Open a lemonade stand?"

"Maybe you and Smoak could run something together."

"Fuck you Belle."

Sabella giggled over the dig.

"Hmph, the only thing we'd ever run is away from each other." Sabra went to study herself in the mirror.

"So did we put on these things to stand around and gripe or are we going swimming?" Belle asked once she'd selected a gauzy black coverup.

A Lover's Origin

"Mmm..." Sabra twisted before the mirror and frowned. "I think I'm gonna put on that peach bikini."

"Sabi...We've been up here over an hour and *now* you wanna change?"

Sabra threw up her hand and went to look for the bikini in question. "We all can't have hips and thighs like *you* Belle. This thing makes me look straight as a board."

"Really?" Sabella tilted her head to take in the overabundance of bosom and behind her cousin possessed.

"Just hush, it won't take me a minute to change." Sabra cursed when the suit wasn't among the clothing littering the lounge chair she'd taken possession of. "I don't even know why I care- it's not like any of Q and Quay's stupid but sexy friends'll be down there to drool over us."

"Oooh... my babies..." Catrina Ramsey didn't care if her *babies* were six foot plus college seniors; no one was going to tell her she couldn't fawn over them like a mother hen. Standing on her toes, she drew them both into a hug and squeezed their necks tight.

Quest and Quay didn't mind. In unison, they turned their faces into the crook of their mother's neck and inhaled her scent which never failed to comfort them.

Once the three-way embrace had ended, Catrina went to hug the young man who had arrived at the house with her sons.

"Sweetie..." Catrina leaned back to cup his face. "I'm so glad you decided to spend some time with us."

"Thank you Miss Catrina." Isak 'Pike' Tesano's tone was as soft as his obsidian stare.

A Lover's Origin

"I spoke to your mother," Catrina patted his chest. "I was so sorry to hear about your grandpa Liam. You give your brothers and the rest of your family our condolences, you hear?"

Pike's faint smile triggered the dimples on either side of his mouth. "I will Miss Catrina."

"Fuck this shit," Quay headed for the spiral staircase beyond the foyer of his parent's Seattle home.

Catrina couldn't quite make out the exact phrase Quay had muttered before he stalked off. She knew it wasn't anything nice and looked to his twin for answers.

"I'll explain later." Quest promised.

Catrina studied Quaysar as he stalked up the stairs and then slid another warning stare toward her first son. "Isak's room is right next to yours. Why don't y'all go on up and get settled in?"

"Yes ma'am." Quest' response was eager. He was more than grateful for the reprieve from his mother's questions.

***

"Hey Q? I'll wait for your downstairs, alright?" Isak was done with his unpacking and went to see if his frat brother was ready to leave for the pre-season Seahawks game they were heading to that evening.

"Yeah, I'll be just a sec!" Quest's voice resonated from somewhere in the depths of his bedroom.

Pike took his time heading down. He strolled the corridor leading toward the spiral staircase. The wall was lined with framed portraits and miscellaneous snapshots of family. Pike couldn't help but feel comforted by what he felt in that moment. His grandfather Liam's death had

A Lover's Origin

dropped his family into a state of chaos. More appropriately, Liam Tesano's death had dropped the family into a *deeper* state of chaos.

The serenity stemming from the picture lined corridor was waning. Nothing ever really did the trick there anyway. Pike wondered if he'd recognize serenity if it walked up, introduced itself and slapped him in the face. Little did he know that he was seconds away from finding out.

Sudden giggles and rumbling interrupted the quiet of the corridor. Two tall dark young women chattered away as they sprinted from one of the guest rooms. Intrigued, Pike followed them at a snail's pace. They were incredible to look at, even though he hadn't caught a glimpse of their faces yet. Their bodies... their bodies were the things X rated fantasies were made of.

Sabella snapped her fingers. "Shoot, I forgot my cover up."

Pike watched as the girls turned unexpectedly as if to head back up the staircase. He recognized one of the beauties as Sabra Ramsey. The other he'd never seen before, but she... she struck him. It was as though she had literally struck him the second she looked at him. For the first time in... ever, he recognized it. Serenity had walked up, introduced itself and slapped him full and hard across the face.

"Hey P?! Hold up, man!" Quest caught sight of Pike in the hallway.

"Come on Belle," Sabra called, slapping at the plump line of her cousin's thigh.

A Lover's Origin

With effort, Belle looked away from Quest's friend. Forgetting about her cover up, she followed Sabra downstairs.

Pike was down the stairs and outside walking toward the pool before he'd even realized it. He found Sabra already lounging across the brick patio, smoothing what he assumed to be sunscreen across her bare arms and legs. The other was nowhere in sight. Sabra had called her Belle. She must have called her Bella, Pike thought. She was the most incredible thing he'd ever seen.

There was a splash and then he saw her taking the steps leading up from the pool. Intrigue heightened, he strolled closer. His onyx gaze clung helplessly to the ample, appealing expanse of her thighs and derriere. He was almost envious of the water beading against her pecan brown skin.

Belle stopped on the ladder, squeezed water from her hair and blinked it from her lashes. She gave a start when she saw a pair of white Adidas in her line of sight. She made her way out of the pool and smiled when she recognized the guy from upstairs.

"Hi." Her soft voice was even softer in light of the curiosity he'd roused.

Pike could only nod at first. He knew how idiotic he must have looked gawking at her that way but he couldn't help it. The pecan brown of her complexion enticed him as fully as the lush provocative curves that made up her frame. He watched her dry the hair that was the same rich brown as her skin. The mass hung down her back like streams of wavy ribbons.

A Lover's Origin

"I'm Isak. Isak Tesano."

She blinked, all too familiar with the last name but she smiled just the same.

"I'm Sabella-"

"Belle?!" Quay was making his way across the patio then.

"Hey..." Belle held open her arms and gave her cousin a tight squeeze when he pulled her close.

"Q's lookin' for you." The harsh intent had returned to Quay's pitch gaze when he addressed Pike.

"Right." Pike fought to hide his grimace while observing Quay's arms about Sabella's waist.

"Right," he sighed that time. This one was definitely off limits, he realized. "Nice meeting you Sabella."

She nodded, her expression unknowingly flattering as her eyes lingered on his incredible bronzed features. "Nice meeting you." She managed.

Pike allowed himself one last lingering look, raking his black stare over her in one heated sweeping motion. Quaysar clearing his throat signaled an end to the enjoyment.

Quay rolled his eyes when Pike finally walked away. "Punk ass. Ow!" He cringed when Belle punched his chest.

"What's wrong with you? He seemed real nice."

"Mmm hmm. Bunch of pretty boys..."

Bella watched Quay in disbelief. "Well if that ain't the pot callin' the kettles black!"

Quay shrugged. "Did you happen catch his last name?"

A Lover's Origin

She shrugged. "You can't hate him for who his brother is. If that was the case, Quest wouldn't have a friend in the world."

"Funny." Quay tugged her damp hair.

"Goin' to get a Coke Belle. You want one?!" Sabra called as she left her lounge chair.

Belle went back to drying her hair. "Bring me a water!"

"You can bring *me* the Coke!" Quay called.

Sabra stopped mid-stride and frowned. "You're staying?"

"Thought I would." Quay settled onto a vacant lounge chair. "Unless there's no men allowed?"

Sabra grinned. "*Men* are always allowed. Little boys on the other hand…"

"Y'all stop." Belle ordered through her giggles. Her two cousins could bicker like an old married couple once they got started. "Quay won't you miss out on the game? I heard aunt Cat say something about Quest going to see the Seahawks."

"Screw that shit." Quay leaned back in the lounge and closed his eyes. "Aint in the mood to hang tonight with Q and his frat *bruh*."

"Hey kids! We're cooking out in an hour!" Catrina called from the screen deck.

Sabella, Quay and Sabra waved and enjoyed their time at the pool without further conversation.

***

Pike went looking for Sabella the second he and Quest got back from the game that night.

A Lover's Origin

It wasn't very late but Sabra had already turned in. Pike didn't dare knock on the door to the room the girls were sharing and cursed his poor timing.

He thought he'd done a pretty good job of pretending to be interested in the game. Truth was, he couldn't get Sabella out of his head. It made no sense. Sure she was the most incredible thing he'd ever seen, but was it her looks alone that had him acting so dumbfounded? Or was it that need for peace and serenity that had him hooked? Was it the promise of peace and serenity that lurked in the deep pools of her warm eyes that had him mesmerized?

He stopped in his tracks, realizing his muddled thoughts had led him out to the pool. There, found her.

Belle looked up a moment after he'd approached her lounge. It was as if she'd expected to see him there and that was more than a little unnerving.

"Quay's gonna kill me." His voice was a whisper.

Belle smiled. "He doesn't like you very much but I don't think he'd go that far."

"Hmph." Pike reached out to rub a lock of her windblown hair between his fingers. "When I tell him that I don't give a damn if you're his girl or not, he'll definitely try to kill me."

Belle didn't know if she felt more amused or shocked. "The twins are my cousins." She managed finally and watched in disbelief as his ebony gaze turned even more bottomless.

"Cousins?" Pike sat on the nearest lounge.

"Sabella Ramsey." She offered her hand for him to shake.

A Lover's Origin

He took her hand to hold instead. His fingers stroked her palm, his eyes followed the path of his touch.

Sabella felt something respond inside her and it almost made her moan. Gently, she pulled her hand free and swallowed when he looked at her.

"Why don't I know you?" I've been Q's roommate for over two years." As if he were helpless to stop it, his ebony gaze raked her face and body draped in a simple yet alluring gold lounge dress. "Thought I knew almost everyone in his family."

"I'm not in college." She set her hands in her lap and studied them.

Pike nodded. "So you live here in Seattle?" He was desperate to make conversation and purge his mind of thoughts of them doing more than talking.

"I live in Paris."

That caught him off guard. "Paris?" A hint of laughter tinged the word.

Belle even had to giggle. "I'm in school there. Um…design school."

Pike bit his lip for a second. The gesture added a more adorable quality to his looks. "What kind of design?"

She bowed her head. "You'll laugh."

He raised a hand. "I swear."

It was Belle's turn to study him then. She wasn't one to fall into a stupor over a guy's looks especially not when she'd grown up witnessing the way women made fools of themselves over the men in her family.

But this guy… he'd been on her mind since she'd seen him on her aunt and uncle's staircase. She thought she'd heard every adjective there was to describe beauty.

A Lover's Origin

She was wrong. There had to be more. Hell if she could think of any, but this guy was most definitely beautiful and then some.

He was tall with the kind of lean build that allowed him to make anything he wore look good. Given his mixed heritage, his complexion was a rich bronze tinged by copper. The coloring was offset by cropped waves of glossy blue black hair. Eyes dark as crude oil were set deep beneath thick straight brows. Mmm hmm... this guy was beautiful and then some...

"Bella?" He was waiting for an answer to his question.

"Um," she cleared her throat and grimaced over her reaction to him. "Fashion. Fashion. I um, want to design clothes." She nodded when he had the decency to appear really impressed. "You can laugh. Everybody else in my family did when I told them."

He was already shaking his head. "I don't want to laugh, Bella."

She looked away again, having never cared for that particular shortening of her name. *Bella-* Italian for beautiful. She'd never felt close to that. Ever. When Pike said it... Lord where had he come from?

"Is that your dream?" He was asking.

"For as long as I can remember. When it was time for college, my mom said she'd rather see me follow my dream than waste four years trying to get a degree I'd never use."

Pike's dimples spliced his cheeks deeply when he laughed then. "She sounds like a smart lady."

A Lover's Origin

His voice was like a whisper that she didn't have to struggle to hear. "She is." Belle sighed and ordered herself out from under the spell he'd weaved around her. "I should go."

"Can I call you sometime?" He dropped his hand across hers when she braced it against the arm of the lounge.

"Why?" She watched his hand smothering hers.

"Because I want to know you."

"Why?" Faint laughter tinged *her* voice that time. She couldn't even look at him.

Pike blinked as though he'd just discovered something vital. The girl had no idea how incredible she was. He'd been in awe of her since he met her and she had absolutely no clue of her appeal.

"May I call you Bella?"

"Quest has my numbers." She blinked, stunned by the reply she blurted. "I should get upstairs. Sabra's been having bad dreams since-" She winced.

Pike didn't need clarification as his mood soured then. "I'm sorry."

Belle's luminous brown gaze softened and she tilted her head to study him. "You didn't have anything to do with it."

"Smoak's my brother." He shrugged. "That's enough for some."

"Not for me." She told him and then eased off the lounge before the moment turned intense again. "Good night Isak."

A Lover's Origin

He clenched fists to keep from pulling her back. "Goodnight." He said when she was already back inside the house.

***

Following a restless night of sleep, Pike woke before dawn the next morning. Sleep had been a joke- a string of torturous dreams of the hard-core variety featuring he and Sabella Ramsey. Laps in the pool until he keeled over sounded like a good idea. He set out before the house stirred.

Apparently, someone else had the same idea. Pike heard the shower shut off in the small cabana where he'd gone to hunt for a towel. Before it occurred to him to leave, the bathroom door opened and Belle emerged.

She was tucking the flaps of a bath sheet around her breasts and didn't tune in at first to the fact that she wasn't alone.

Pike swallowed, once again cursing poor timing. Patiently, he waited for her to take note of his presence and smiled when her eyes finally met his.

"Sorry." His whisper-soft voice seemed to echo in the room.

Belle walked closer toward him. She kept her arms folded over her chest as if that would deter him staring at the swells of her breasts above the towel.

"Thought I'd catch a swim before anybody else got up." He explained.

Sabella cringed. "Sorry, I had the same idea too. I try to um…take a lap every morning."

A Lover's Origin

"To wake yourself up?" Pike moved closer to where she stood near the sofa.

She smirked. "To lose weight."

"What the hell for?" He blurted, angry then that she didn't see herself the way he did.

"Have a good swim." She moved for the door.

He was blocking it by the time she got there.

"Isak…"

"Mmm hmm?"

She made one last attempt at leaving and next found herself pressed against the cabana door. His knee between her thighs prevented any movement.

"Quay and my uncle Damon will kill you if they find us here." Her voice shook more with desire than warning.

"Guess I'll have to chance it." He was kissing her before the last word silenced.

Sabella could have slid down the length of the door had his knee not been there to stop her. Helplessly, she ground herself against him there, silencing any voices that even hinted at chanting words of caution.

She'd wanted to test the texture of his hair and once her fingers were lost within the onyx waves, she found them to be as satiny as she'd imagined.

Pike didn't care how weak his whimpers made him sound. He'd wanted to kiss her since he saw her, wanted to test the sweetness he knew lingered within her mouth. Her full lips beckoned to him as strongly as every other part of her. His hands flexed around the towel covering her, but her grip upon it doused any attempt to tug it free. He moved his hand to cup one generous swell then and succeeded in weakening her grip on the towel.

She was trembling all over by the time he ended the kiss. Her mouth was trailing the line of her neck, both hands squeezing, weighing her breasts as he applied faint brushes to her nipples from the tips of his thumbs.

Every part of her tingled, sizzled or screamed for his attention. Somehow, common sense intervened and she fought to tamp down those other more stimulating cravings.

"Isak... Isak, stop." Weakly, she'd been grasping the forearms that were corded with muscle. Her hands curved into fists which she set against his chest. "Stop Isak."

Unable to ward off her command, Pike inhaled the scent of her skin one more time before he stepped back.

Sabella couldn't look at him and felt her need battling against her common sense. Then, anger stepped in to lend a hand.

"Did your brother tell you us Ramsey girls were good for giving it up if you pressed the issue?"

Pike blinked, clearly stunned by the question. Belle frowned unable to believe the words have actually left her mouth.

"No Bella. That's not why I did that, I swear it."

She was too ashamed of herself to even look his way. "Let go." She asked.

He did without hesitation. He watched her leave as every part of him fought against going after her.

The next day was filled with activity. The foyer of Damon and Catrina Ramsey's home was littered with

A Lover's Origin

backpacks, suitcases, basketballs and random pairs of sneakers. The group was preparing to head back to school in California.

Sabella would ride back with Sabra. Her trip wouldn't end in San Diego, but go on the Monterrey where her mother lived.

Breakfast had been an informal affair. Catrina set out a mountain of chicken and egg biscuits, hashbrown wedges, juice and coffee and told her guests to have at it. Belle was grateful the morning wouldn't start with a meal where she'd have to exchange tense looks with Isak Tesano the whole time. Following her accusation the other morning, the rest of the day was frustrating at best. Sabella hid out in the room she shared with Sabra. Unfortunately, the romantic suspense thriller she'd cracked open couldn't keep her mind (or her body) off the devastating Tesano that had come into her life.

She regretted her words to him in the cabana especially after telling him he wasn't to blame for his brother's actions. Now she realized she'd been desperate and had uttered the first stupid words that came to mind. The guy made her nervous- that was obvious but he also made her suspicious. What could he possibly want with her? She guessed he was curious, his brother had certainly had his world turned inside out by her cousin. She figured Isak was just looking for a similar experience.

That thought didn't completely convince her, but she wouldn't allow herself to believe he was actually interested in her. With looks to die for and a body to match, what could he possibly want with her? As usual, she cast off reminders of all the boys who'd come knocking upon her door in the past. They professed interest as well but she never gave them the chance. She'd become a pro at cutting down suitors, but this one... this one hadn't slipped in unnoticed. Isak Tesano had made his presence and his intentions known and she hadn't done a thing to stop him. She didn't *want* to do a thing to stop him.

Belle dropped her last case into the back of Sabra's BMW and turned... right into Pike. His hands came up to steady her, but he didn't actually touch her. Swallowing notably, he eased his hands into the back pockets of his sagging jeans.

"I wanted to apologize for yesterday morning Bella."

"Don't. Please, you apologizing only makes me feel worse."

"Jesus," his smile was sad as he winced. "I can't do anything right by you, can I?"

"No," she moved closer and unconsciously rested her hand on his arm. "No, it's me. I acted like a jerk yesterday. I shouldn't have said what I did."

"I didn't mean to make you feel that way." His bottomless eyes searched her vibrant brown ones as though he were trying to find a way beyond them.

Belle smiled up at him. "You didn't make me feel *that* way." *You made me feel unreal.* She cleared her throat. "I just-"

"Belle!"

Quay's roaring didn't stun them. Pike and Belle experienced similar reactions. Simultaneously, they bowed their heads and smiled as though they'd expected some type of interruption.

A Lover's Origin

"I should go." She said.

Pike didn't relinquish his spot near the trunk. "May I still call you?"

"Sabra's ready." Quay was slamming down the hood of the trunk then.

"Thanks Quay." Belle sang and then turned her head in her cousin's direction but didn't look his way. "You can go now."

Quaysar gave Pike the benefit of a menacing glare before doing as his cousin told him.

"Quest has my numbers." She reminded him once they had a measure of privacy.

Pike's dimples emerged faintly as the beginnings of a smile tugged his mouth. "Is that a yes?"

Belle watched as Sabra headed to the car, stood near the hood and glared at her along with Quay.

"It's a yes." She said and then left his side without another word.

***

As a member of the Ramsey family, surprise and downright devastation were given emotions. Sabella didn't believe she'd ever been more surprised than on the snowy Saturday afternoon when she opened the door to her tiny Paris flat and found Isak Tesano in her hallway.

"You said… you said you'd call." Belle couldn't hear above her heart thundering in her ears.

Pike shrugged. "So I did."

Her almond brown stare was wide and searching. "What are you doing here?"

A Lover's Origin

"Freezing," he pretended to shiver beneath the black three quarter length leather jacket he wore. "You didn't tell me it was going to snow this weekend."

"You didn't tell me you were coming."

His deep gaze narrowed with knowing intent. "And have you leave for Thanksgiving break before I could get here?"

She smiled. He'd come to know her pretty well over the last two and a half months. This in spite of the fact that their 'involvement' had only been by phone.

Pike moved to lean against the paint-chipped doorjamb. "Are you gonna let me in or leave me to freeze out here?"

Sabella figured he wouldn't be freezing for long. Already, her nosy female neighbors were lingering in the corridor or peeking out their doors to size up the sexy specimen who'd come to call on her. She stepped aside to let him enter.

"The apartment's small," Belle was saying as she put her shoulder against the door to help it close properly. "There's not a lot of room so-"

He was right behind her when she turned.

"It could get tight." She added.

Pike's smile was wickedness personified. "That's what I'm hoping for." His last word was silenced seconds before his tongue enticed hers into a kiss.

"Mmm..." Belle was in danger of sliding down yet another door. Again, his knee between her thighs prevented that. Again, she ground herself there already sizzling with the need he could rouse by doing little more than speaking to her.

A Lover's Origin

She wasn't dressed for visitors. He took full advantage, finding his way beneath the tie-dyed T-shirt she wore with a pair of sweats. "Wait... God, wait..." she murmured while kissing him desperately.

Surprising them both, Pike ended the kiss. He'd hoped they could save conversation for later, but; as he'd shown up with no warning...

Sabella blinked when he backed off and then took advantage of her sudden freedom to slip out from between him and the door.

"Sorry I showed up like this." He removed his jacket and then took his spot against the door. "Did you have plans?"

She laughed. "No. No plans."

Pike took a look around the apartment. She didn't lie when she said the place was small. Still, it erred on the side of being cozy instead of confining. Clearly, she had a touch for making a home.

"How much time do you spend here?"

"All of it when I'm not in class." She smiled and headed for the even smaller kitchen off from the living room.

Pike followed. "Bet everybody else was jealous as hell when you got to go away to Paris for school?" He smiled when he heard her laughter that time. Full and amused... and real.

"Sabra didn't speak to me for a week. Coffee?" She asked when Pike appeared in the doorway. "Why are you here, Isak?" She asked when he nodded.

A Lover's Origin

"I told you," he shrugged and looked down at his sneaker shod feet crossed one over the other. "I wanted to catch you before you went home for the holidays."

"Why me?" She focused on preparing the coffee.

"Why not?"

She feigned interest in wiping down the countertop. "Don't tease me."

Pike's mouth fell open at her nerve. She'd been teasing him since he met her. His gaze faltered and he clenched his fists on the need to lose his fingers in the wavy ribbons of her mahogany brown hair. The curves she possessed…they beckoned him like a spoken word. He couldn't get her out of his head. The way she felt next to him, had stoked the possessive streak that he thought he hadn't inherited from his father's bloodline. Sabella Ramsey had no idea how tightly her fate was sealed.

"You asked if designing was my dream." She'd turned from the sink then.

He nodded.

"My *dream* has always been to be a size four." She smiled. "I'd settle for a ten. Girls size twenty-two and up have to settle for simply *designing* clothes that size, I guess." She went to take two mugs from a cabinet. "You could have anyone you want, you know that. I've got a hall full of neighbors who'd tear your clothes off as soon as look at you."

Pike couldn't help but chuckle over her prediction.

"So?" She challenged, her gaze unwavering then as she watched him. "Will you at least tell me why- one reason why…? Why me?"

A Lover's Origin

"Bella, Bella..." Pike pushed off the jamb and crossed the minute distance that separated them. "We could waste all afternoon talking about the reasons why." He toyed with a lock of her hair that had fallen loose from the French braid she wore. "Lucky for me you only asked for one."

He surprised her when; in one fluid motion, he set her atop the counter she'd just wiped down. Sabella felt her T-shirt whip over her head and instinctively moved to cover herself. Pike was having none of that and closed his hand over both her wrists to hold them captive against his chest.

"Isak..." Was all she had time to utter before his tongue was filling her mouth. Weakly, her fingers curved into the knit fabric of the black turtleneck he wore. Her need for answers drifted into oblivion and eagerly she participated in the kiss.

Confident that she'd settled in her mind the inevitability of them making love, Pike released her wrists and set about the task of undressing her. Her taste was like some drug that he'd become hopelessly addicted to. His hands faltered more than once, weakened by the effect of their dueling tongues.

Belle curved her hands into the high collar of his sweater before inching upward play in the luxurious thickness of his hair. She could hear herself moaning and didn't care how it made her sound.

More arousing than what his hands and mouth were doing to her, was his awesome strength. She was no lightweight, but damn if he didn't make her feel like a feather when he took her from the counter and into his

A Lover's Origin

arms. She felt totally safe against him-secure in the power he held over her body and mind.

As her miniscule apartment only consisted of three rooms; the bathroom notwithstanding, Pike needed no directions to her bedroom. Lucky for Belle. She was far too absorbed in kissing him senseless to even think of talking.

She'd also been far too absorbed in kissing him to realize that he'd removed every scrap of clothing she wore. Suddenly, she was all too aware of what was happening and her self-consciousness set down like an anchor.

"Mmm mmm," Pike wouldn't allow her to reach for the small flannel blanket that lay across the bed.

"The light." Her voice trembled and she looked toward the small lamp on her nightstand.

Instead, he rose above her and pulled the sweater over his head. "If you think I flew all this way to grope around in the dark, you're crazy."

"I've never..." She couldn't tell him that she'd never gone so far with anyone.

The dimples flashed as his gaze narrowed. "Good." He whispered, the possessive streak shifting into overdrive then. Yes, this girl had most definitely sealed her fate.

Sabella bit her lip on the intensity of the desire she saw lurking in his deep stare. When he dipped his head to kiss her, she melted- done with arguments and excuses.

Pike used the tip of his nose to trail the curve of her jaw and satiny line of her neck and collarbone. It traveled the abundance of her bosom until she writhed next to him in a show of impatience. A shuddery moan lilted from her throat when his tongue outlined a firming nipple, his thumb tortured the other with faint, stimulating brushes. Sabella felt a slow stream of need dampen her inner thigh.

"No…" She sobbed when he abandoned her nipples to journey on to continue his intimate exploration of her body.

Tentatively, she delved her hands into his blue black hair. She pushed the wavy locks from his forehead trying to observe his expression looking for any signs of disapproval. If there was one, she couldn't detect a hint of it. What she saw instead was something awe-filled, curious and; if she didn't know any better, worshipping.

Sabella's eyes widened when he suddenly pulled away again. This time, it was to doff what remained of his clothing. Belle bit her lip on a moan when he tugged away the T-shirt he'd worn beneath his sweater.

In a state of awe then herself, she reached out to rake her nails across the array of muscles carved into his torso. The shade of his skin was like burnished gold with the power of the sun reflecting against it.

A small affected cry resonated from her throat when he lay upon her again. Sabella shivered; not from any chill of the outdoors seeping past her windows but from the sheer pleasure of his taut bronzed body against hers.

Pike cupped her cheek and favored her with another thorough kiss. He murmured her name each time his tongue caressed hers. Sabella's participation in the kiss then was tentative at best. So many new experiences, all so unexpected and with a guy she'd never seen coming… overwhelming indeed.

His mouth sought the base of her throat and nibbled at the pulse beating there. His pleasure providing lips

A Lover's Origin

moved onward to lick and suckle her nipples equally lavishing his attention to both. Belle realized he was moving away again and she caught his wrist before he could get too far.

"My jeans." A hint of laughter colored his words.

Belle watched him slowly pull a few condom packets from his back pocket. "So few." She noted with a playful sparkle in her eyes.

"Well I couldn't shove 'em all in my jeans," he tossed aside the garment and opened one of the packets. "What would the customs people say?"

"What a thoughtful guy you are." Belle curved her hands over his shoulders when he settled against her once more.

"Then I should tell you," his expression sobered. "You may not like this part very much."

"What par-" Belle shrieked then as an unexpected and intolerable wave of pain sliced through her.

Pike let his head rest in the crook of her shoulder once he'd claimed her virginity. He winced having heard the shriek when he lunged forward inside her. Taking her slow would have only caused her more pain. He wanted that over and done with so that she could enjoy everything he wanted to do with her.

"Wait," Belle's hands had curved into fists when the pain lanced through her. Somehow, a more subtle sensation was working its way through the discomfort of the invasion and it enticed her hips into movement.

Pike groaned into her shoulder when he felt her tightness clutch and then release his length. That time, it was *his* fist clenched against the sensation overtaking him.

A Lover's Origin

His desire-induced responses knew no bounds as he growled them into her skin. His hands encircled the lush expanse of her thighs, opening more of her to his thrusts.

Belle pressed her head deep into the pillow while curving her nails into the taut flesh of his chest. The chiseled pects flexed beneath her touch and she arched her breasts against him in response.

Pike kept one thigh a bit higher than the other, increasing the penetration of his sex inside hers. His hair brushing her skin; as he lowered his head to her breasts, felt like she was being stroked by mink. Belle kept one hand clenched within the glossy black mass while the other lay weakly above her head.

His throbbing stiffness stroked her to climax. At the same time, he fed from her nipples suckling one while his fingers fondled the other.

Gradually, Belle's moans gained volume and wavered amidst the potent arousal he'd ignited within her. She was trembling then as the unfamiliar stir of an orgasm took its placed at the heart of her.

Pike raised his head to watch as she gave herself over to what was happening. Her lovely eyes were closed and her lips were half parted to make way for her sighs. When the erotic spasm possessed her, she bit down on her bottom lip to relish the sensation.

To Pike, she was a mix of provocative innocence. He couldn't tamp down the desire rampaging through him when her need flooded against the sensitive sheet of the condom. He gave into what his body demanded then and increased the depth of his lunges. He let go of her thigh and

A Lover's Origin

laced his fingers between hers while pressing her hands to the covers beneath them.

Belle draped her long legs around his back and met his thrusts with a force of her own. Pike was muttering something in the crook of her neck where his gorgeous face was shielded from view. Another few seconds passed and then she felt him become even more rigid inside her if that were possible.

The growls that had been surging from Pike's throat sounded like the low rumblings from a drum then as his hunger was satisfied for the time being.

Sabella waited, not quite sure what was to happen next. Contentment staked its claim within the intimacy as Pike slowly withdrew, curved her into his powerful frame, nuzzled her head against her chest and drifted off to sleep. Belle followed his example moments later.

"Why does everyone call you Pike?" She asked hours after their naps had ended and they'd made love again.

He was chuckling, indulging in the feel of her hair teasing his fingers. "My uncle Pitch gave it to me."

"Pitch?" Belle shook her head against his chest. "Forget I asked." She smiled at the feel of his laughter vibrating against her ear.

"Now I've got to tell it." He spent a few more seconds chuckling. "My uncle Pitch is my favorite uncle. He never had any kids of his own, so he always went overboard whenever he came to visit us. Took us fishing all the time- even during the winter."

A Lover's Origin

Belle propped her fist to his chest and set her chin on top of it. "I've never been fishing."

The obsidian depths of his gaze softened as it studied her face. "I'll have to change that, won't I? Anyway," he tugged on a lock of her hair. "He came to visit one month and we went out together just the two of us. I caught this fish... thing had to be as big as I was. I told uncle Pitch that Hill and Smoak would never believe I caught it. They didn't, but after my uncle finished the story of how I caught it, they couldn't do a thing but stop callin' me a liar." He chuckled again on the memory. "He gave me the nickname because that's the type of fish I caught and he never called me anything else but Pike. He said it'd always remind everybody about what I'd done." He shrugged a bit. "My uncle Pitch is a *huge* guy- big intimidating- a take no shit kind of guy. My dad told me he always wanted to be like him when he was little and so did I. The nickname made me feel like I was."

"Sounds like you had a great childhood."

Something dimmed in his gaze, but he smiled. "For the most part. My family and my brothers are great, the rest of my family..."

Sabella laughed and pressed her fingers to his mouth. "I get it, trust me."

Pike suddenly turned the tables and flipped her beneath him. "When I leave here, I won't have sex with you again until you're my wife."

The unexpected turn towards intensity rendered Belle speechless for the better part of a minute. "You're crazy."

He grimaced. "Certifiably."

A Lover's Origin

"You could have anyone."

He gave her a quick jerk and brought his finger to the tip of her nose. "Make that the last time you ever say that to me."

She blinked. "But you could." Her voice sounded small and faint.

He smiled. "And you're it. So I guess this means you won't be arguing with me anymore, hmm?"

"You don't know me." She closed her eyes against the thoughts that were making her dizzy. "We don't even know ourselves yet."

Pike couldn't help but laugh again. "You've got tons of these excuses, don't you?"

Her expression was subdued. "Mmm hmm."

He settled himself intimately against her. "Then let's get this out of the way first and you can finish listing every single one of them."

"Will you listen to me?" Her lashes fluttered as he probed the part of her that ached and yearned for him.

"I'll listen," he murmured against her ear.

She gasped when he was nestled deep. "Will it make a difference?"

"Not even one." He promised and silenced all other conversation with a kiss.

A Lover's Origin

Yohan and Melina

Hampton, Virginia~

    The cozy feel of Yohan Ramsey's off campus apartment had nothing to do with the fact that the Christmas holiday season was in full gear. The four bedroom dwelling was always beautiful and inviting. Yohan never allowed his surroundings to look anything less than pristine, but there was an added appeal to the environment that evening. The place teemed with cozy soft lighting and provocatively mellow jazz that seemed to have been piped into every room. The delectable aromas from the meal Yohan had prepared topped off the relaxing aura of the evening.

A Lover's Origin

"I don't know if I've got room for that dessert you're about to bring out." Melina Dan's tilting gaze harbored a playful glint as she observed her boyfriend of over two years across the round table they shared.

Yohan's resulting smirk was accompanied by the slow rising of his sleek brows. "We'll see," was all he'd say.

Melina's fork paused over the last of the spectacular stir fry. With effort, she tugged her eyes away from Yohan's fierce dark features and looked toward their college in the distance. Through the fresh sprinkling of snow, she could see lights twinkling in the distance causing the campus to resemble a tiny city. She'd been so absorbed in the view beyond the bay windows in the living room that she hadn't noticed Yohan leaving the table. He returned moments later with a tempting Key Lime pie.

Melina shook her head and sent heavy tufts of her coarse hair bouncing against her cheeks. "Is all this an early Christmas present?" She asked.

His low chuckle seemed to echo in the room. "Uh-uh."

"So what made you do all this?"

"No big deal," his deep black gaze shifted toward her face to capture the disappointment that had fallen into place there. "You okay?" He began to cut the pie.

Mel shrugged, rubbing her arms across the sleeves of the blue knit sweater she'd worn for the evening. "Just wondering… what's going on with you. Are you about to dump me or something?"

His laughter roused full and heartily then.

"Maybe you're trying to let me down easy."

A Lover's Origin

He finished with the pie and watched her closely. "Why would you think that, Meli?"

"You're a Ramsey." She cleared her throat, remarking on the connection she'd only recently made. "Why waste time with one when you could have many." Melina didn't realize how angry she'd made him until he'd shoved his hair back from the table.

"I'm not like my family, Mel."

She frowned, thinking it was a strange thing to say but dared not to question. He looked angry enough to kill. "I'm sorry." She whispered and looked back toward the campus. "We just… we've never talked about *exactly* who you are… it's just weird that you never talk about them."

"Hmph. Not weird if you know 'em."

"This looks so good." Mel focused on the delicious pie fearing their light cozy mood was on the verge of growing dark.

Yohan watched her for several seconds before rejoining her at the table. For a while, the only sounds in the alcove were of silverware scraping dessert saucers.

"You should meet them." He said when they were on their second slices of the pie. "My family." He clarified when she'd stopped chewing. "You should meet them."

A tiny spring of happiness welled inside Melina. She'd been on pins since her cousin had told her just who she was dating. Of course her first question had been why a guy like him would be interested in an exclusive relationship with one girl. In truth, the fact that he was a Ramsey had little to do with it. Melina could practically feel the jealousy rolling off other girls whenever she walked by on Yohan's arm. The boy could've had anyone-any number of *any ones* off his looks alone. He was dark, powerfully built with fiercely gorgeous features and he was intelligent. The looks warranted more than a passing glance, but combined with the intelligence...

"You'll probably not want to see me again once you meet them."

Melina blinked, feeling her temper heat over his self-pity. "Yohan listen. I've known who you are and even more about your family for a while now. Johari Frazier's my cousin."

"Johari." Yohan recognized the name of his brother's girlfriend.

Mel didn't bother to hide her amusement over his reaction. "Jo's dad and my mom are twins."

Yohan was slumped back against his chair. "Jesus..."

Melina helped herself to more of the pie. "Didn't take long to figure you don't like talking about your family. I didn't want to upset things."

"Because I'm a Ramsey?" He asked while massaging the bridge of his nose.

Melina pursed her lips. "Jo says your folks seem like nice people and; coming from my cousin, that's sayin' a lot."

"Hmph. She and Moses haven't been together that long."

The certainty clinging to his slow deep voice sent a shiver along her spine. "This pie is incredible. Let's just eat, alright? It's probably not a good idea to talk about your family after all."

"You'll have to meet 'em sooner or later, Meli."

A Lover's Origin

  She laughed over his persistence. "Well there's no rush, is there?"
  "There is, if you're going to marry me."
  Somehow, she managed to swallow the rest of the pie. "You're asking me to marry you?"
  "No." He smiled, watching another wave of disappointment take shape on her exquisite molasses dark face. "I plan to though. But I won't let you go into it before you meet 'em."
  "Yohan..." She slumped back against her chair then too. "You make them sound like the devil."
  That familiar twinge of anger curdled again inside Yohan and again he left the table. "You're not far off," his voice was a growl. "Dead on the money as far as my dad goes." A quick surge of deep humorless laughter rose from his chest then. "Funny that I'd say that when I'm my dad's favorite. He tells me so every time I talk to him."
  "Han..." Melina stood recognizing the affect the conversation was having on him.
  "Can you believe that shit?" Yohan was too bogged down in his thoughts to hear anything else. "Like it makes me feel good to know that he hates my brothers?"
  She rushed over then, stepping in front of him and squeezing his face. She gave his cheek a light slap to make him look at her. "Stop this, do you hear me? Stop." Melina shook her head, her exotic slanting stare raking his face with blatant appraisal. "I've seen evil, Yohan. I've *seen* it." Her hold on his face, firmed as memories surged of her unexpected visit to the scene of a crime years earlier. She dismissed the thoughts and graced Yohan with another smile. "No one like that could make someone so

A Lover's Origin

incredible." She smoothed the back of her hand down his flawless cheek.

His need for her never lurked too far below the surface. Driven now by never-ending frustrations over his family and a building wave of emotion for her, he leaned down to kiss her deep.

The intensity of his tongue plundering her mouth would have frightened Melina but she was too determined to soothe the temper quietly raging inside him. The sweater she wore was soon a memory as were the matching bell-bottomed slacks and chic platform boots which only added a few inches to her minute height.

She was chilled by the air brushing her skin while Yohan carried her to his bedroom. Clothed only in her underthings, she was eager to feel him bare next to her.

Inside his room, he tossed her to the mammoth sized bed set on a platform in the corner. Melina tried to slow her breathing as she looked upon him. The fierce magnificence of his features took on a more basic element. She swallowed with effort as the intensity of his expression affected her.

Boldly she pushed off her back and went to kneel before him on the bed. He stood there watching as she took charge of undressing him. His inherited streak of arrogance was heightened by the adoration in her stare as she peeled away his shirt.

As she often did, Melina actually moaned at the sight of him. Sure he'd been her first, but the sheer size and powerful sculpting of his form would affect the most... *experienced* woman. She let her nails travel every carved

A Lover's Origin

inch of his torso awed by the way the muscles flexed beneath his molasses drenched skin.

Deftly then, she tugged away his belt and was pulling him down to her as his jeans and boxers fell to the carpet. She kissed him hungrily; moaning each time her tongue caressed his.

Yohan tried to call on the restraint he kept heightened when they were intimate. She was so unbelievably small, he feared causing her a second's pain.

Melina wasn't interested in restraints and precautions that night. She was terrified by the fact that he was so unnerved by his background to the extent that he'd believed she'd leave him over it. Words could only go so far in convincing. Melina was of a mind to use her body to show him that he was the man- the only man. That sort of convincing wouldn't happen overnight but that night would be a good start.

"Mel..." Yohan's voice was muffled where his face hid against the crook of her neck. He realized he was practically crushing her in the embrace and would have moved back were it not for her legs tightening around his back.

"No Han please..." She pressed against his hands, urging him to maintain the pressure of his hold.

"Melina," his voice held a warning chord. His restraint was approaching the nonexistent mark.

She arched close and began a slow suckle of his earlobe, breathlessly chanting his name as she rubbed against him.

"Hell," Yohan took her suddenly and without thought to protection. He winced on the pure pleasure of being inside her; without their usual barrier of precaution. He'd only indulge in a few seconds, he promised himself.

Those seconds, were approaching the minute mark and Mel wasn't helping him to interrupt the moment. Weakly, he called her name, hoping she'd snap to and assume the cooler head. She wasn't of a mind to do that if the rolling of her head back and forth against the pillows and flicking of her thumbs across her nipples were any hint.

Yohan treated himself to a few more lunges, knowing he was dangerously close to spilling his seed into her. He growled another curse squeezing her bottom with intentions of withdrawing.

She muttered something incoherent, but it stifled his intentions to break their contact. Instead, Yohan brushed her hands from her breasts. He covered one nipple with his mouth while his fingers took over the role of manipulating the other.

The triple wave of sensation had Melina laughing breathlessly and savoring the ecstasy claiming her. Eagerly, she met his thrusts giving him no cause to be concerned that he was hurting her.

Without warning, Yohan turned the tables and took on the submissive role. His dark incredible gaze did not falter as he absorbed the sight of her caught up in the intimacy they shared. Her hips moved in an erotic twist that had him clutching her bottom again with intentions of pulling her off his erection before he came.

"No." she covered his hands with hers and pulled them up to fondle her bosom. "Mmm…" To torture him for even thinking of stopping, she slowed her movements almost to a halt.

A Lover's Origin

Yohan tugged her down and feasted on her nipples again. He outlined her full, pert breasts with the tip of his nose before resuming the hungry suckling again. Infrequently, he muttered commands to his hormones, urging them to cool just a bit. She felt like heaven inside and he wanted to remain right where he was for as long as he could.

The interlude did eventually reach its conclusion. With thoughts of protecting her his top priority, he again moved to tug her from his ever tightening shaft.

"No…"

"Mel I should-"

"No," she suckled his earlobe again. Deliberately, she brushed the tips of her breasts, still wet from his attentions, across his chest. "Come inside me," she whispered.

His groan was torture personified. Her words were like part of some hypnotic suggestion he had no choice except to obey.

Melina shuddered, biting her lip on the sensation of the warmth flooding her then. Instinctively, she clenched her sex round his, relishing the massage that stroked her core.

Once they crested on the waves of satisfaction, they attempted to catch their breath upon a shore of contentment. Deep sleep was next on the agenda. Still, intimately connected, they drifted off into oblivion…

***

A Lover's Origin

Seattle, WA~ Christmastime...

Marcus and Josephine Ramsey's yearly holiday celebration was more for business networking than family time. Melina enjoyed it all whatever the reason for the elaborate gathering. Attire was semi-formal and she delighted in observing the women decked out in the most stylish outfits.

Melina even had the opportunity to chat with her cousin for a few moments. Johari was on her way out of the party though with Moses who stopped to talk with Mel for a few moments before whisking his girlfriend into the snowy night.

Fernando was next to make his exit from the party. Like Moses, he also stopped to chat with Mel before heading out the door with three girls clinging.

"Don't ask." Yohan urged Melina when she pointed towards Fernando and his entourage. "Someone I want you to meet." He said, tugging on the sleeve of her crimson coatdress while turning her toward a woman who stood a few feet away.

"Mama this is Mel," Yohan cleared his throat and took his mother's hand as he pulled her close. "Melina Dan." He said and smiled at the sparkle in Josephine's eyes. "Meli this is my mother Josephine Ramsey."

Melina's smile was genuine albeit shaky. "It's nice to meet you Mrs. Ramsey." She extended her hand.

Instead of a quick shake, Josephine held onto Mel's hand. "And *very* nice to meet you, sweetheart. My son was right. You *are* exquisite."

A Lover's Origin

"Thank you Mrs. Ramsey." Mel bowed her head on the compliment and then looked up and motioned toward her surroundings. "Your home is just as exquisite- even more so."

Josephine looked around her home and the people, furnishings, artistry and holiday décor filling it. "It's been a fulltime job, putting it together and *keeping* it together with four men rampaging through it, I'm afraid."

"Well you do a great job." Mel was saying once their laughter had quieted.

Josephine was still holding Melina's hand. She gave it a quick shake. "Would you like a tour?" She asked.

"I'd love one." Mel blurted, her excitement taking over.

"Don't look so down, baby." Josephine called over to Yohan. "We won't be long."

Yohan felt far from down. The way his mother had taken to Melina warmed something inside him that he never knew existed.

"I'll meet you in the dining room." He told Melina and graced her with a wink before she walked off with Josephine.

The *dining room* was actually a separate buffet room opened especially for the many soirées given by Marcus and Josephine. Four long tables curved through the candlelit room with its sparkling chandeliers fixed in the high ceilings. Small round tables were set along the carpeted edging. Guests could enjoy their food at the tables or return to other parts of the house to mingle.

A Lover's Origin

    Melina hadn't met up with Yohan since returning downstairs from her tour with Josephine. The house was, in a word, spectacular. Given the added holiday decorum throughout, the place seemed even more magical.
    Not to mention the food, Melina thought as she piled another of the spinach filled mini-quiches to the saucer she balanced on her palm. The tiny plate already held an obscene amount of delectables from the buffet. Surely she could fit just one more of thing, Mel decided. Her attempt proved to be the wrong move as the addition of the last quiche caused the rest to tumble from the saucer.
    "Oh shit," Mel hissed, her cheeks flaming with embarrassment as she watched the food liter the pristine maple hardwoods beneath her feet. Glancing quickly across her shoulder, she knelt to gather what had spilled.
    "There love, don't worry about that. Someone'll be along soon to clear it."
    The voice that touched her ears sounded as deep and reassuring as Yohan's. It wasn't her boyfriend, Melina realized when she stood to thank the man and froze.
    Marcus Ramsey didn't take note of the reaction from the young woman who watched him with wide exotically slanting eyes. One word from him quickly brought a server over to clear the food from the floor.
    "See?" Marcus turned to smile at Melina. Then, he froze as well.
    Melina didn't realize she was backing away until she felt her way blocked by a solid wall of muscle.
    "There you are." Yohan brought his arms about Mel's waist to keep her tight against him. "How'd you like

A Lover's Origin

the house?" He asked, while brushing his mouth across her cheek.

Mel opened her mouth to respond. There was no sound.

Yohan realized why and laughed once he'd followed the line of her gaze. "Oh, hey Pop." He gave Melina a nudge. "Marcus Ramsey, Melina Dan."

Marcus managed to overcome his surprise and put a charming smile in place. "So this is Melina. Very nice, son." His dark beckoning gaze raked Mel in one sweeping, appreciative stroke. "Very nice." He extended his hand. "Pleasure to meet you darlin'. It's a lot of work getting my son to talk about anything else except you."

Melina had to send a conscious note to her brain to extend her hand. "Mr. Ramsey." Was all she could manage when her palm touched his.

"Ramsey!"

Both Marcus and Yohan looked in the direction their last name was called. It was another of Marc's associates waving him to join the group of men chatting in a far, smoke filled corner of the buffet room.

Marc threw up his hand, and then winked at his son and nodded toward Mel. "Very nice meeting you, sweetness. Yohan, you show this pretty thing a good time, hmm?"

"Not a problem, Pop." Yohan grinned as his father strolled off toward his associates. Several seconds passed before he realized that Melina had not moved.

"Hey?" He squeezed her hips, giving them a proprietary pat before tugging her back next to him. "You okay?"

A Lover's Origin

"I..." Melina closed her eyes in hopes of absorbing some of his strength. "I didn't realize how much Moses looks like your dad."

Yohan chuckled. "Yeah... Mo hates when people tell him that. Ma says he's the spittin' image of Pop he was a kid."

"Jesus..." She had to bury her face in her hands then.

Yohan squeezed her again. "You sure you're okay? My dad can be a lot to take first time you meet him."

"I'm fine, I promise I... Guess I need a little sleep."

"Hell, I'm sorry babe." Yohan's expression relayed regret. "I wasn't even thinkin'. Ma's got a room ready for you. I know she was hoping we'd stay the night instead of going back to the hotel."

Melina stifled her groan. As incredible as her surroundings were, she wanted nothing more than to get the hell out of there. Still, Josephine Ramsey had been so very gracious and Mel really did like her a lot.

Yohan was offering his arm. "Take you up?"

A loud roar of laughter burst from the table in the back of the room. Mel shivered and reached for Yohan's arm as if it were her lifeline.

***

Marcus Ramsey. Marcus Ramsey, could this be any more unreal?

That had to be it, Melina thought as she paced the plush bedroom that had been especially prepared for her. It was unreal, she thought. It had to be. In what sort of reality did one of the most powerful men in the country take part in the rape and murder of a highschool girl?

A Lover's Origin

Shivering then, Mel rubbed her hands up and down the sleeves of her gray chenille robe. Idiot. A *naïve* idiot-that's what she was. Powerful men did perverted things all the time. What made this particular reality seem so *unreal* was the fact that *this* powerful man happened to be her boyfriend's father.

The knock on the door almost forced the waiting scream from her throat.

"Meli?"

"Han." Relief almost brought her to her knees. "Coming." She whipped open the door without thinking to close her robe.

The smile he gave sent his devilishly dark eyes narrowing. "For me?" He reached out to draw one side of the robe further away.

"Not in your parent's house, it isn't." She closed the garment over the bra and panties she wore.

"Girl if you only knew the things that have gone on *and off* under this roof."

Mel rolled her eyes. "I can imagine." She moved back when he stepped past the doorway. "No Yohan."

He shut the door and locked it.

She kept her robe closed with one hand while extending the other in warning. "No Yohan."

He took her hand and pulled her flush against him.

"Yohan I'm saying no."

He kissed her, chuckling softly just before his tongue slid inside her mouth. It took no time at all for him to entice her into becoming an enthusiastic participant in the act.

A Lover's Origin

"I'll make it quick, I promise." He said during the kiss.

By then, Melina was hoping that was a promise he wouldn't keep. Eagerly, she moaned when he tugged her high against him and carried her to the turned down bed.

Intent on keeping his promise, Yohan didn't bother with taking her out of the robe. He left her bra in place as well but tugged the lacy black panties from her hips. As for his own attire, he simply unfastened his trousers and freed his sex from its suddenly tight confines.

He pleasured her with a stunning oral treat, draping her legs across his shoulders as he nuzzled between her thighs.

Melina found that her voice had deserted her when she tried to cry out. She had no control over her body which behaved with a will of its own, thrusting back against Yohan's tongue as he drove it relentlessly.

Before she could come down off the climax he'd roused, his impressive erection was buried to the hilt inside her. Melina lost strength in her hands and could only let them fall to rest on the pillows cradling her head.

Her body opened to anything he desired, Yohan took her with an intimate hunger. Dropping wet soft kisses to her bare skin, he finally paid homage to her breasts. His lips and tongue bathed and suckled her nipples which strained beneath the fabric of her bra.

Melina bit down on her lip desperate to silence the pleasure-induced cries lodged in her throat. When his grip tightened to a crushing hold on her hips she sobbed her disappointment. He was coming heavily and she wasn't far behind.

A Lover's Origin

    Yohan took a few moments to catch his breath before he kissed Mel's shoulder and raised up over her. Frowning playfully, he checked his wristwatch.
    "Twelve minutes. Quick enough, huh?"
    Mel grazed her nails along the fierce array of muscles carved into his abdomen. "What are you doing?"
    He smiled, loving the weariness clinging to her voice. He leaned down to nuzzle her ear. "Keeping my promise," he whispered. "While I can." He added, and then fixed his clothes and tucked her into bed before he left.

    ***

    Sleep visited quickly for Melina the night before, thanks to Yohan's very attentive visit. Morning arrived all too soon though. With it, returned the thoughts of Marcus Ramsey and the vicious gleam in his eyes when he and his friend savaged that poor girl.
    Mel woke early, dressed and headed downstairs. Fresh snow was falling on the first day of Christmas week. The crispness of the air finished waking her as she took a walk around the grounds.
    She returned to the house some forty minutes later and claimed a chilly spot on the balcony overlooking the back of the estate. From her perch along the balcony's brick ledge, she studied the enormous Christmas tree-one of four the house boasted. Melina tried to lose herself in the magic of the twinkling multi colored lights. They mesmerized her enough to soothe her troubled thoughts for a time.
    Whatever was troubling her though, was still very visible to Yohan. He'd watched her trudge up the back hill through the snow. As she sat staring morosely; a something

A Lover's Origin

that should have at least sparked a grin, he cursed himself for bringing her there.

"Hey," Melina's smile emerged when she saw him coming out to the balcony.

Yohan offered no response until he was leaning next to her along the balcony. "I love you." He said.

Mel pressed a cold kiss to his jaw. "I love you too."

"I think I made a mistake bringing you here."

"Han." She frowned and turned to face him. "Why?"

He shook his head "Don't know. A feeling."

"No Yohan." She covered his gloved hands with hers. "I'm glad you brought me. I guess…being around your folks is making me miss mine. I usually go along whenever my dad sees his family in China." She shrugged beneath her hunter green overcoat. "I'm just a little down about it, that's all."

Yohan tugged up the brim of her hat in order to look deeper into her exotic stare. He seemed convinced and gave another slow nod.

Melina nudged his shoulder and frowned playfully. "What?"

"Just um," he pulled a small square velvet box from his pocket. "If I do this…"

She gasped when he opened the box.

"And if you tell me no, I'll be crushed." He teased.

"Han…" the gleaming diamond rivaled the snow for brilliance. "Are you sure?"

"Am I sure I want you to be my wife? Right now it's the *only* thing I'm sure of. What I'm not sure of is whether you want to be."

A Lover's Origin

"Do I want to be?!" She gushed and then pressed both hands to her mouth to tamp down the happiness about to turn her inside out. "I want that more than anything. I love you so…" Her words silenced on the kiss she planted to his mouth.

"Meli… my family-"

"Shh… soon they'll be *my* family too."

Yohan looked ready to laugh. "I wish there were a way to explain to you what that means."

"I don't care." She eased off the ledge and came to stand before him. "As long as it means you're my husband."

He pulled the ring from the box while she pulled the snowy glove from her hand.

"Will you be my wife Melina Dan?"

"Forever Yohan Ramsey," tears pressed her eyes when he pushed the band onto her finger. "Forever," she promised.

A Lover's Origin

Caiphus and SyBilla

  A gorgeous peach satin gown lay across the deep carpeting along with a matching pair of chic pumps which were overturned and half hidden beneath a three quarter length tuxedo jacket. A crisp white shirt and black trousers were slung across the bench at the foot of a stately king bed. Unmentionables of the male and female variety draped the carved pine footboard- panties and boxers entwined with hose and a lacy peach bra.
  The bowtie for the gentleman's tux was draped about SyBilla Ramsey's neck just then...
  "They're gonna kill us... mmm..." She bit her lip on the stab of sensation that staked her someplace deep.

A Lover's Origin

Caiphus Tesano spared a second to brush his mouth across the beauty mark at her inner thigh. "Would you like to go down?"

SyBilla laughed at his phrasing, then gasped when he resumed his nibbling on the folds of her sex. "I've already gone down. It's your turn." She moaned and felt his body shake as he chuckled.

Caiphus was taking 'his turn' quite seriously. He'd spent the course of the last week trying to woo the tiny temptress into bed. Now that he had her there he was of a mind to enjoy every minute.

SyBilla wasn't interested in controlling the volume of her cries. They mingled with her moans, filling the room with sounds of pleasure.

"Shh... You want them all to know we're up here?"

She couldn't give her response. He'd pressed her thighs further apart and drove his tongue deep.

"Hmm?" He encouraged an answer while rotating his tongue inside her sex and brushing his nose across the hypersensitive bud above it.

The double caress sent SyBilla's cries into overdrive. She clutched at the cottony soft dusky blackness of his hair. Insatiable then, she moved her thighs back and forth across his face loving the feel of his baby soft skin.

"Mmm..." her trembling cry gained another level of volume.

"Yes..." she snuggled deeper into the tangled bed and screamed when he brought his fingers up to toy with her nipples.

A Lover's Origin

"Fuck it." Caiphus growled then, realizing that her enthusiastic cries would soon bring the entire wedding party into the room.

"No…" SyBilla quieted when he withdrew.

It was only to grab his discarded trousers and get the condoms from the back pocket.

"Caiphus please…" SyBilla didn't care if she was behaving like some passion drugged idiot. The man had stoked a fire only he could douse and she needed him to tend to it without further delay.

Protection was soon in place. Caiphus tugged her to the middle of the bed, his sinfully appealing features were unreadable when he draped her leg across his shoulder.

SyBilla threatened to draw blood from her lip when she bit down on it. By length and width, he filled her completely and she prayed climax would remain at bay- at least for a while.

Intent on silencing her throaty cries while silencing his hormones that demanded conquest, Caiphus brought his mouth down on hers. SyBilla's moans were effectively muted as she drank her moisture from his tongue.

Then, it was Caiphus whose moans threatened to bring notice to what they were doing. She was so incredibly small and unbelievably tight. She gloved his sex in such a way that it defeated any ability to hold back the release building at the tip of his shaft.

"Bee," he groaned into her shoulder after breaking the kiss. "Jesus…" he winced, the needs of his body overwhelming his mind. His fingers flexed at her hip as his thrusting slowed. For a time, he relished the sensation of being sheathed inside her.

A Lover's Origin

SyBilla couldn't be still. She moaned softly while gliding her tongue along the powerful chords in his neck. Slowly, she ground her hips against his while clenching her inner walls about his erection.

Caiphus muttered something incoherent and resumed his driving thrusts. He came so powerfully then, that SyBilla could feel the pressure of it against the condom he wore. The sensation brought on the climax she'd been holding back since he put his mouth on her.

They lay entwined for several moments after. Bill was first to rouse, thankful that Caiphus appeared to be sleeping. She tried to slip from the bed unnoticed and found herself trapped by the arm that had snaked about her waist.

"Caiphus..." she turned expecting to see his extraordinary turquoise stare.

He was asleep though and had subconsciously reached out to keep her close. *Hmph, probably not used to having a woman leave his bed until he tells her to.* Bill mused, then made another careful attempt to go. She collected her things and quickly dressed, keeping her eyes on him as he slumbered.

Soon, she was ready to leave the room but hesitated. Moving close to the bed again, she took a moment to study him. His features, relaxed in sleep were even more magnificent. She wouldn't curse herself or call herself an idiot for going to bed with him. Hell, what woman could resist such an offer? Tentatively, she reached out to brush her thumb across the curve of his jaw. Intrigued all over again, she savored the feel of his skin- flawless and soft as a babe's. Men so gorgeous were dangerous, she reminded herself. After all, she'd grown up around a ton of them. She

A Lover's Origin

knew firsthand how arrogantly they selected and then discarded women who flocked to their beds in droves.

Her beloved sisters/cousins had already fallen victim to two of the devastating Tesano brood. She pulled her hand away from Caiphus' face and grimaced. Previous actions notwithstanding, she didn't plan on being more of a *victim* than she'd already been. She'd been curious, that was the jist of it. She'd never sleep with him again.

Content with that decision, she placed his bowtie on the pillow and left the room without looking back.

When the door closed, Caiphus opened his eyes, pressed the bowtie to his nose and smiled.

***

"...You know I just never know when they'll make contact and I have to be ready for it anytime- for their calls... what?" SyBilla frowned at the look her cousin was giving her.

Sabra shrugged. "Just tryin' to figure out why the hell you're tellin' me all this?"

Bill rolled her eyes. "So you didn't happen to notice that I wasn't around while our cousin took her wedding vows?" She snapped, her slate gray stare narrowed and furious.

Again, Sabra shrugged.

"Was Belle mad?" Bill wrang her hands and looked around the lively reception hall.

"Please," Sabra rolled her eyes that time. "That girl is floatin' on cloud ninety-nine with Pike Tesano on the brain."

"Well..." Bill gave a nervous tug on her gown's bodice. "We *were* her maids of honor, you know?"

A Lover's Origin

Sabra flagged down a waiter and exchanged her empty champagne flute for a full one.

Bill winced, watching the girl down over half the glass' contents in one swallow. "So um... what about *your* Tesano on the brain?"

"Son of a bitch." Sabra paused from drinking to say. "Didn't even bother to show up to his own brother's wedding. Sent some pitiful gift to make up for it. Triflin' ass…"

"Excuse me? Bee?"

SyBilla closed her eyes at the sound of his voice. She was partly mortified by the fact that she'd actually have to speak to him again after they… The other part of her was aroused all over again. His voice wasn't very deep and held a softness that was unexpectedly persuasive.

"Sorry Sabra, for interrupting."

Sabra waved a hand, more intrigued then by the wilting look on her cousin's face. "Not a problem." She said, biting on her thumbnail as she grinned over the realization that dawned.

"Can we talk for a minute, Bee?"

Figuring a 'talk' with Caiphus Tesano would be less painful than a round of twenty questions from Sabra, Bill nodded.

Instead of asking whether she wanted to dance, Caiphus simply guided her toward the floor. Closeness was the last thing Bill wanted. That's what she told herself anyway. It did no good to press against his chest to keep some bit of distance between them. He kept her snug against him.

"Can't you look at me, Bee?"

A Lover's Origin

It was either that or keep her eyes on the bowtie which roused erotic images best forgotten. Looking up into his face didn't make the situation any easier. Focusing on his lips and the cleft chin beneath them only encouraged thoughts of where his mouth had been. Keeping her gaze on his chest only made her think of his toned frame bare next to her in the bed they'd shared. She'd only be able to think of the rich copper toned skin stretched taut over his leanly muscled frame.

She'd focus on his eyes, stunning turquoise orbs where the element of playfulness and something a tad darker lurked. The pair of gold rimmed glasses he wore made him look like the clean cut young man next door. It didn't take long for a girl to discover though, that the nice young man image was a front for the sex connoisseur waiting to pounce.

"Hope you enjoyed that before." SyBilla decided leaning on her hardness would be the only way to resist what he stirred inside her. "I don't plan on being a repeat customer."

His lips twitched but Caiphus didn't dare let her see him smile. "Repeat customer?"

"Well I'm guessing you wanted to complete the set. Your brothers have already had my cousins. I'm sure you wanted to know what all the fuss was about."

He groaned. "Bee..."

"Caiphus." One of three young women leaving the dancefloor stopped to speak.

"Be sure to save me a dance too." The young woman practically moaned the words.

A Lover's Origin

    Caiphus simply offered a smile which he held while the women lingered and stared with unmasked heat.
    SyBilla wouldn't have been surprised to see the little fan club come out of their clothes. "Here, why wait?" She said then and extracted herself from Caiphus' loose hold. She left him on the floor with his admirers.

***

    "Does all that hardness help, Bee?"
    SyBilla bowed her head when she heard his voice. She looked away from the late evening downtown Seattle view, but didn't turn and give him the benefit of her gaze.
    "I'm not about to make more of this than it was." She said.
    Caiphus came to lean against the opposite end of the terrace railing. "And what was it?"
    "We gave in and we screwed." She looked at him then. The slate gray intensity of her eyes was steady. "No more to it than that." She suddenly shook her head. "What do you want with me anyway? I'm not some tall busty goddess with hair down to my ass like my cousins."
    Floored then, Caiphus could only observe the little beauty before him. It was written all over her face, she really had no idea how provocative she was. He knew nothing he could say would change her mind about that fact.
    "So why did you sleep with *me*?" He asked instead.
    "Curiosity." She smiled over the admission. "My cousins don't just give it up to anyone in spite of what your brother may've told you about Sabra." She laughed shortly and turned to look back out over the view. "Guess I wanted

A Lover's Origin

to see if you were worth giving up a moment of my dignity for."

Caiphus pushed off the rail and moved closer to Bill. "Just so you know, Smoak hasn't said a thing. Nothing negative, that is." He tilted his head to look at her then. "Did you ever ask yourself if maybe I was curious too?"

Her laughter rose fully then. "I know you were curious!"

He grimaced and pulled loose his bowtie. "Not about that- not about what you were like in bed." *Beyond satisfying*, he said to himself and figured it was best not to share the opinion. "Maybe I'm curious about you Bee- you *out* of bed."

"Why?!" She looked stunned.

Caiphus laughed then too. "You've got no idea what Belle did to my brother. Threw him for a loop and that's putting it very mildly. As for Smoak... the guy's pitiful... sick to death over what he did to Sabra. He's a mess."

"And you want that kind of drama?"

"My dad always says nothing worth having ever comes easy or fast." He moved closer to where she leaned against the rail. "Women come to me very easily little Bee."

"And I just proved that, didn't I?" She smiled.

"But you say you won't sleep with me again." His bright stare lowered to rake the appealing swell of her bustline... "That's a problem for me," he sighed and brought his eyes back to hers. "I'm afraid it's not something I'm used to."

"Can't you just live off the memory?"

A Lover's Origin

His laughter flavored the damp cool of the evening. "No Bee. Not when the memories are that good."

SyBilla chewed her lip and debated on sharing her next words. "Quay says your family is a group of criminals."

Caiphus closed whatever distance rested between them. "And what do *you* say?" He smoothed the back of his hand across the satin bow at her waist.

"Nothing yet." She took a moment to inhale deeply of the appealing scent of his cologne. "I have a job though which could require me to find out one day." She looked up and let him see the certainty in her gaze then. "That could wind up being a problem for you too."

"I'm not worried." He slanted her a sly wink.

"That's because you're very young."

"Ha! And what are you? Eighty?"

SyBilla rolled her eyes. "I've got at least five years on you."

"Whoa... you're really ancient." The teasing light left his vibrant stare then. "I intend to have you the same way my brother has your cousin."

She blinked and studied him in disbelief. "You're crazy."

He locked her against the rail, one hand on either side of her. "Is that a problem for you?"

"It won't ever happen." She shook her head, missing the way his eyes followed the healthy bounce of her short wavy hair.

"You're devastating in bed," she admitted, raising her brows when he appeared surprised she'd confess such a

A Lover's Origin

thing. "Unfortunately, you'll never be devastating enough *out* of it to keep me interested."

Caiphus only smiled, the turquoise brilliance of his eyes confirming that he recognized her challenge.

"You offered and I accepted." SyBilla went on, dismissing how intently he studied her. Reaching out, she tugged on the bowtie hanging loose then around his collar. "Let's just leave it at that, hmm?" She pressed a lingering kiss to his cheek, brushed her thumb across the seductive curve of his mouth and left him there on the terrace.

The smile never left Caiphus' face. He touched the spot she'd kissed. "No way in hell, little Bee. No way in hell." He watched, until she was out of range of his stare.

The End

Dear Reader,

Thanks so much for diving a little deeper into the Ramsey world. This effort was a recent idea that came to mind. I realized that there was just too much backstory (especially with the Tesanos) to put into a prologue. I also wanted to give a bit more story on the couples you already know and love. So much of what is known about them is based on dialogue and memory sequences in the main titles so I wanted to add a bit more to close the gaps.

I do hope you've enjoyed this effort. I'd love to hear your thoughts, so please drop me a line anytime: altonya@lovealtonya.com

A Lover's Shame coming March 2011.

Peace and Blessings,
Al
www.lovealtonya.com

An AlTonya Exclusive

Made in the USA
Lexington, KY
03 February 2011